THE FLOWERING

by Agnes Sligh Turnbull

NOVELS

The Rolling Years
Remember the End
The Day Must Dawn
The Bishop's Mantle
The Gown of Glory
The Golden Journey
The Nightingale
The King's Orchard
Little Christmas
The Wedding Bargain
Many a Green Isle
Whistle and I'll Come to You
The Flowering

NONFICTION

Out of My Heart
Dear Me: Leaves from a Diary

FOR CHILDREN

Jed, the Shepherd's Dog
Elijah the Fish-Bite
George
The White Lark

VOLUMES OF SHORT STORIES

Far Above Rubies
The Four Marys
This Spring of Love
Old Home Town

Agnes Sligh Turnbull

THE FLOWERING

HOUGHTON MIFFLIN COMPANY BOSTON

1972

First Printing c

ISBN: 0-395-13947-3
Library of Congress Catalog Card Number: 72-75613
Printed in the United States
of America

TO MY GRANDSON

JAMES PAUL O'HEARN

WITH MY LOVE

CHAPTER ONE

IT WAS AUGUST and the warm day seemed as exultant as a mother who has a family of children to show for her labors. For here in all the garden beds was a rich profusion of late asters and early chrysanthemums, of roses and zinnias and snapdragons. "Just as though summer would go on forever," Hester Carr thought as she tidied the articles on her dressing table, put on the jacket of her brown linen dress and started down the stairs. She found her housekeeper polishing the dining room table, her favorite piece of furniture.

"I'm off to the hairdresser's, Hattie."

The older woman surveyed the other critically and then said, "Well, it's about time!" as she gave a final survey to the thick auburn hair that *had* grown a bit long.

Hester laughed. There was a friendship between them

more than that of servant and mistress. "All right. I'll come back properly shorn. As you know, I let everything go for a bit now."

"An' it ain't right, as I've often told you. Mr. Walter wouldn't want you to do that. I miss him myself though I know he never liked me, but just because you're a widow . . ."

"Don't!" Hester said. "I've asked you never to use that horrid word. I hate it. I will be a relict, if I have to, or I'll be the late Mr. Carr's wife, but I'll never be a *widow,* so don't say it."

"All right. But I don't see why you're so touchy about it. Plenty women as good as you are widows. They even have a Widows' Club down at my church . . ."

"Hattie!"

"Well, I'll try not to say it but it's mortal hard to keep from it when that's what you *are.* Go along now an' get yourself trimmed up. You look tousled to me."

Hester waved her hand and went on out the door into the warm, richly scented sunshine. She was early for her appointment so she did not hurry. Instead she walked along the quiet suburban street, musing. It was true, as Hattie had insisted, she *was* a widow, that strange feminine entity who had once been endowed with a dual personality and was now only half of what she had been. A certain fulfillment, greater even than physical, had left her. There was a nakedness of spirit, as though the clothing of daily habitudes had dropped from her, leaving her bare. She was a widow, though she would never speak the word, and she was lonely.

In the months since Walter had been gone, and there

now had been ten of them, she had thought deeply of their relationship. They had been quietly, contentedly happy. The lack of children, which Walter did not seem to mind but which she lamented inwardly, had added a certain quiet, even monotonous overtone to their lives. There had never, even at the first, been any delirious or passionate love. She had been young then and did not know enough to miss it. Later the even tenor of their lives seemed to blot out for her any question. Walter's law work had prospered surprisingly, they had indulged themselves in comfortable ways, their home was a place of beauty with inherited antiques and Hester's fine taste in arranging their own new selections with them. Walter's gift had been with the garden . . .

Hester's eyes were misty. He had loved flowers and was even planning for a small electric fountain when so suddenly all life seemed to stop. He had been only forty-five and now she was not even forty. Thirty-six and alone.

A circle of little children were playing "The Farmer in the Dell" as she passed one of the larger lawns. The echoes followed her all the way until she reached the turn for Main Street.

The cheese stands alone, the little voices chorused in the climax.

"It's the wife," Hester thought. "It's the wife that stands alone."

That night as she sat at the polished table with Hattie serving her meticulously, the while she injected a remark now and then, Hester found to her consternation that two tears had slid down her cheeks before she could stop them and in another moment, she supposed, would be in her soup. The thought made her laugh, though the attempt was shaky, and Hattie had already been a witness to the weakness.

"I don't know what's the matter with me," Hester said. "I think I may be getting a cold."

"Fiddlesticks!" said Hattie. "It's no cold. You're lonely, that's what you are an' I've been givin' a lot of thought to it. I think, Miss Hester, you've got to have something in the house besides me. Something to pet. I think you ought to get a dog."

"A *dog!*" Hester exclaimed. "Why what on earth do you mean?"

"You know perfectly well what I mean. One of them animals on four legs that wags its tail an' barks. Now let's be serious."

She leaned on the back of the chair that used to be Walter's. "Your husband left you well fixed. You know that, Miss Hester. An' all you've got to do is read the paper an' you'll find out all the awful robberies an' murders an' such that's goin' on. Now my point is, we're two lone women here. A dog would be company for you an' me too, for that matter, but it would protect us. I've read that a barkin' dog's worth a dozen door locks. Now, Miss Hester, I want you to think this over real careful an' I'll bring in your dinner now."

Hattie had achieved part of her general purpose. She had roused her mistress from her apathy until a tear seemed an entirely foreign substance. In fact Hester could hardly wait to discuss the matter of the dog further, though she told herself it was quite out of the question for her. Walter had never cared much for dogs; neither had he approved of Hattie's casual remarks during dinner but they had always amused Hester and now she gave hearty thanks for them.

"But, Hattie," she began now, as her dinner was placed before her. "I know nothing about dogs except that they really are quite a care. A dog has to be *walked* every day and . . . and bathed and brushed and oh, I don't know what all. I couldn't possibly undertake such a responsibility."

"An' who's askin' you to do it alone? I've just told you I'd like a dog myself, haven't I? An' I'm sure I'd feel safer with one in the house. Just last night" — she lowered her voice — "I woke up with a bangin' on the back door. It give me a startle. I come down without wakin' you till I'd see what was goin' on."

"What was it?" Hester asked, fright in her voice.

"Oh, it was just the wind blowin' that dead cherry-tree branch against the porch roof. It ought to be cut down. I've told you before about it."

Hester laughed. "So there was no burglar or any interloper at all."

"Not *this* time," Hattie put in quickly. "But you can't tell what it might be another night. As I say, we're two lorn females here an' the things you read make my hair stand on end, I'm tellin' you."

Hester lifted her hand lightly to indicate the conversation was ended. "Now, Hattie, I think we're quite safe and can get along nicely just as we are, so don't go scaring me with stories that have no foundation. Just think," she added, "how muddy paws would put tracks on your polished floors! Let's just forget the dog."

Hattie muttered darkly all the way back to the kitchen, another little habit Walter had tried in vain to break, and Hester went into the living room where after roaming about for a few minutes she sat down at the grand piano and was soon lost in the music.

It had, indeed, been her solace and joy over all the years of her wifehood, which had begun soon after her year of college. Her father's remarriage, too soon, Hester felt, after her mother's death, to a woman she disliked, and the quiet, implacable attentions of Walter, then twenty-five, with his feet firmly planted on the first rungs of his own particular ladder, had seemed to make the early union inevitable. Life with Aunt Cissie, who had befriended her, still left her uncertain of the future. Her college year had been a disappointment. She felt she could do better with her music in private study. Walter was strong, eminently eligible and determined to have her; Hester was insecure, hurt already by life and afraid, so they were married. Sometimes, as she came upon old pictures of her girlhood, she apologized to herself for the vanity but admitted that without knowing it then she had come near to real beauty. The thick, wavy auburn hair, the wide-set gray eyes which even in the pictures seemed to have a light in them; the singularly sweet smile. Walter had been proud of her looks. He never complained over her dress bills. Once, she remembered, when he was eyeing her proudly as they were dressed for a party, she had said, "I wonder whether it is my appearance you love or the real me inside it."

"Why, it's all the same thing."

"Not quite. Just imagine if I took, oh — I don't know — smallpox, for instance, and my so-called good looks were ruined, would you still love me?"

"Nonsense!" he had answered. "What a morbid thought."

But Hester recalled that she had lain awake a long time that night thinking about it and not feeling comforted. The worst of it was that she couldn't analyze her feelings properly, even when the small stab she felt in her heart refused to go away.

Now, when she had finished several etudes of which she was particularly fond, she leaned over, her elbows on the edge of the keyboard, thinking, then suddenly she went to the phone and dialed the number of her closest friend. She often wondered how she would *live* if Ginny Masters ever moved away. They were completely different and, perhaps because of that, complemented each other in a most satisfactory fashion.

"She'll probably be out," Hester said aloud as she waited. But she was not. "Ginny . . ."

"Hester," an ebullient voice came, "anything wrong? You never call me in the evening. Down Sandy! Down boy! He always wants to get his nose into the receiver. Well, what's on your mind, lovey?"

"Ginny, the most ridiculous thing has just come up. Hattie thinks we ought to get a *dog!*"

"*Hattie* thinks! So I suppose now that the oracle has spoken you'll get one. Didn't I tell you six months ago that was the thing for you to do? You merely laughed at the idea.

You really make me very mad the way you kowtow to Hattie. Well, you have my blessing, if that's what you're after."

"No, Ginny dear, don't get huffy. It's advice I want. You see I'm not really sold on the idea at all but I wondered if you know a place where I could go, sort of the way one would do in a dress shop, and look over some puppies and come away if I didn't like any, which I probably won't. Where did you get Sandy?"

"Oh, he just dropped from heaven on us, for this man in the office told Bill practically in tears that they'd gotten him and his wife wouldn't keep him. Wasn't she a devil? So Bill just snapped him right up. But listen, Hester, I know the very place for us to go looking, for I'm coming too. I can't wait."

"But I'm really shaky over the thought of all the . . . the care and everything. Don't you push me, Ginny."

"I won't. I promise. But I went with another woman once out to this absolutely *divine* estate where they have kennels way at the back. It's a beautiful drive and we can lunch on the way out. Then you can look at the pups and do whatever you want. And when you are bringing it home, snuggle it up against you. It will be more scared than you are."

"There you go," Hester said. "I can't trust you. I think I'll give the whole thing up before I get into something I'll regret."

"I'll stop for you tomorrow morning at eleven and don't be a goose," Ginny said. "It's the only free day I've got this week so grab me while you can," and she hung up the phone.

9

Hester walked to the door, her heart beating fast. In all the years, she had never had a pet, and the thought of a dog with its demands upon her seemed as strange as though she were considering the adoption of a child. She sighed. That's what she had wanted to do in the past but Walter wouldn't hear of it. He had never been at all eager for any of the various pets she had suggested. "A pretty little kitten now," she had said once. "A tom. That would be fun and practically no trouble!"

"My dear, a pretty little tom kitten has a way of turning into a yowling tomcat. And they *do* scratch the upholstery," he added.

Hester sauntered slowly down the curving walk to the street. A dog *would* be company, she mused. For more and more she found herself alone in the evenings. She and Walter had led a pleasantly busy social life. He enjoyed parties so there were many dinners in their own home and in those of their friends. There were theaters in the city and concerts to which naturally, without giving it a thought, she went escorted. With Walter gone, in spite of the kindness of her closest friends all this was changed. She was the odd woman, or she was left out entirely. The quiet gaiety of the passing years, so long accepted unconsciously, was gone. True, she was still in frequent demand for the daytime bridge parties. These, the girls all said, would be a help to her and brighten her spirits. But oh, the evenings. The intolerable, lonely evenings, when she and Hattie had exhausted their small supply of comments upon mutual interests at dinner and the latter had hastily retired to her room to watch her favorite television program and return promptly at eleven to check all the locks on the doors and windows. But those hours between! Even Ginny, with all her subtle machinations, could produce only an occasional unattached man. And dear soul, Hester thought now with a smile, she was so happily obvious about it that any man in such a position would run for cover. Besides, Hester went on to herself, it seemed too soon for her to be going out anywhere in evening groups, joining in the laughter and the fun. It was still, for her, only surface conviviality, for while the nights were long, the time since Walter had left her seemed short. It was hardly a year.

Now, as to a dog. If she had one she could talk to it. It would be something alive and responsive as the slow hours passed. Of course Ginny was too impulsive and would have to be held down but at least one could think about the matter.

She reentered the house, beat Hattie for once in checking locks and putting out lights and in a short time had prepared for bed. Her room looked inviting with its softly lighted dressing table and muted pink chintzes on chairs and at windows. A quiet haven. Too quiet. She remembered the children on the neighboring lawn that afternoon with their gay little voices as they circled to the game of "The Farmer in the Dell." A birthday party, probably. She thought of the last shrill climax, *The cheese stands alone* — and of her own mental change in the wording. As she got into bed between the sheets Hattie always meticulously opened for her, she once more agreed with her revision. Yes, she thought sadly, it should be, *The wife stands alone.* Then, as she often did as a sort of opiate, she allowed her mind to repeat line after line of rhyming verse. Now it was the words of the silly old game with which she finally drifted off to sleep.

She woke sometime in the night, happily a rare thing now. For a few minutes she tried to recapture the feelings which had brought her something like mirth. Then she remembered. In a dream she had been playing with the children and had at the appropriate time sung out lustily, *The lady takes a dog!* It *was* funny. She drowsed as her unconscious began to take over once again, the more quickly because there was the steady, languorous sound of rain on the porch roof. "At least we'll not be going out to the country today," was her last intelligent thought.

But the next morning was cloudless with the sky a blue which woke the very soul. The grass and flowers, instead of being drenched and drooping, had apparently been refreshed by the shower.

"Well," Hattie remarked as Hester was finishing breakfast, "a fine day for your trip. Now when you're about it, pick a good one that'll be some use to us. Collies are nice, or a German shepherd maybe . . ."

"Hattie, how did you know I was even thinking of going out to look for a . . . a . . ."

"Well, I was in the upper hall last evening and I couldn't help hearing what you said to Mrs. Masters. And I could just about guess what she was saying to you. It's funny but I think she's jealous of me and so was Mr. Walter for that matter," she ended complacently.

"Hattie! You mustn't say such things. If I do go out today it's chiefly for the drive and I may not be interested in getting a dog at all. Of course, I might look at some at a kennel Mrs. Masters knows, but I'm not going to commit myself to anything, so don't get your hopes built up."

"I'll fix up that little orange crate in the cellar with an old blanket. Just in case," Hattie said. "An' I'm glad you're goin' with Mrs. Masters. She's got some gumption." A horn sounded in the drive. "There she is. Well, get along now an' as I say, pick us a good one."

Hester, feeling Hattie had definitely overstepped the line this morning, gave a slight wave of her hand but no more as she left the house. Ginny was busy moving her golden collie to the back seat, a difficult business since he preferred riding in the front. She dusted off the cushion beside her and after directing a few well-chosen words to Sandy, greeted her friend.

"Hester, hello! What a fabulous day! I hope you don't mind a hair or two on your suit. They really won't show on that color. The young rascal did want to come so badly. He loves to ride in a car. So at the last my heart failed me and I brought him. I have his leash and there's always an extra doorman at the restaurant who will hold him or walk him while we eat. He may raise the devil (I mean Sandy) when we get to the kennels but I'll keep in the background with him. Oh, Hester, you're doing the most *wonderful* thing in getting a dog. You'll simply adore . . ."

"I'm not at all sure I'm going to get one," Hester interrupted weakly, and then gave a small scream. The car had all but lurched off the road as Sandy had made an attempt to hurl himself onto the front seat again and nose his head under the wheel. Ginny righted the car, stopped it, put her pet back in his place with a sharp slap and went cheerfully on with the conversation.

"That was a close one. You see he still even at his size wants to sit in my lap. *Down there, you beast, and if you do that again* I'll kill you. You see the trouble is, I love him so much I can't discipline him properly. Tom is better with him of course. But what made it so hard for us was that he was well past the puppy stage when we got him. Now in your case you can start right in at the beginning and it will all be easy. Dogs really *are* so responsive if you . . ."

From the back seat came strange low moans, developing at last with a sharp and steady *Yap! Yap.*

"Oh, dear," Ginny said, "I never can learn sense when it comes to him. I should never have brought him. Would you mind terribly, Hester, changing seats with him? If he's up here beside me he's really very good. Oh, I'm terribly ashamed!"

"That's all right," Hester said. "Stop and I'll do it at once." Mentally adding that anything would be preferable to what had happened so far.

"You're such an angel," Ginny praised, as Sandy took his favorite seat again. "Not *you,*" she added, patting him fondly. "You're a bad, *bad* dog, so there!"

Sandy drooped for a moment at the severe tone, then straightened and watched the landscape with interest.

"I don't mind a bit," Hester assured her friend, "only do watch the wheel."

"He'll really be all right when he's up here and knows I can see him. We're quite close to the restaurant now. It's a sweet place and I flatter myself I discovered it. It's my treat so no arguments. Why yes, here we are. Right there to the left behind the trees. Just hand me Sandy's leash, will you, Hester? It's there beside you on the seat."

But Sandy had seen it first. With a graceful and apparently unhurried leap he had cleared the back of the seat upon which he had been sitting and dived through the opened window behind, which Hester had let down as far as it would go for much needed air — and had forgotten. His beautiful white and golden body was lost in a second among the trees, but alas the ones on the wrong side of the road.

Ginny was white. For once her bright chatter left her. "If I lose him," she kept saying under her breath. "If I lose him . . ."

Hester was then the strong one. "Nonsense!" she said. "You couldn't lose him. He just wanted a good run. Has he ever been to this restaurant before with you?"

"Oh, yes."

"Why don't you drive on in and ask one of the doormen to go with you at least across the road to hunt him? He would remember Sandy."

"Oh, if he'll come at all it would be for me. I'll drive in though and then — oh, it's the road I'm terrified of. I have nightmares seeing him struck by a car. I'm ashamed to be so shaken now, but if he wanders through that woods — and collies always chase cars, you know — if he did start to come out . . ."

It looked to Hester as though Ginny's eyes were full of tears. It was a strange feeling to see her so moved.

"Now cheer up!" Hester kept saying as they turned into the drive. "Everything's going to be all right," admitting to herself as she spoke that she knew *nothing* about such a situation.

They got out of the car quickly, leaving it for the parking man, and Ginny all but ran to the main entrance with Hester close behind. In sight of it Ginny could be seen to clasp her hands in a dramatic gesture, utter a loud and somewhat unholy exclamation. There beside the doorman, sitting in expectant dignity was Sandy. His coat was wet and his paws covered with mud. His tail began to wag violently and his lips to curl in a collie-smile as Ginny rushed to him. He planted both muddy paws on her fresh pink skirt, licked her face and allowed her to rest her cheek upon his head.

"This your dog, ma'am?" the doorman inquired, somewhat unnecessarily, Hester thought.

"Oh yes! And I'm so glad to find him. He jumped through the car window and took off through the woods. I was afraid we'd *never* get him."

"They do that, ma'am. Pretty smart of him to come back here." He reached for the leash. "Want me to keep an eye on him while you ladies have lunch?"

"If you would!" Ginny answered. "I'm sure he'll behave now. Nice Sandy! Wonderful Sandy! Good boy!"

Sandy received the praise as his just due and put one muddy paw on the doorman's immaculate trouser leg as evidence of his acceptance of the new situation.

"I'll make it right with the man," Ginny said when they were inside.

It was a charming place combining rustic overtones with an elusive air of sophistication.

"It makes you purr," said Ginny as they sat down. "Now let's hurry and order for I've something awfully important to tell you."

Once settled with food Ginny leaned nearer her friend. "I wanted to talk to you where Hattie could not be around. She *does* eavesdrop, you must admit."

"I'm afraid so." Hester sighed.

"Well, then, I don't want to scare you or stir Hattie up so she'll be impossible, but have you seen or heard of anything queer in our neighborhood?"

"Mercy, *no!* What do you mean?"

"Now, don't be frightened, but the fact is, there is an unknown man who walks up and down the streets at all hours of the night!"

"Who has seen him?"

"The first were Dan and Bess Hays. They were coming home from a very late party about three o'clock, and they saw this man walking slowly along our street, looking at a house now and then as though he were really — well you know the slang — casing the joint. So Dan and Bess were startled and they notified the police."

"Oh, dear. He may be perfectly harmless."

"That's what the police feel really, but they're not satisfied. It seems they overtook him the next night when he was on the prowl and asked him if they could be of any help to him, for he looked so like a gentleman."

"And what did he say?"

"Why, they said he just thanked them with his lovely English accent and said he always enjoyed a walk under the stars and asked if they had noticed the moon was almost full. Now, what would you make of that?"

"Why it sounds reasonable enough. I like to go out to look at the moon myself."

"But the thing the police didn't like was that he kept his right hand in his pocket and there was a sort of bulge there which they felt *could* be a gun. They are watching him closely. And Hester, doesn't it make you feel queer? And for heaven's sake lock up well. This is one reason I'm thankful you're getting a dog."

"If I am," said Hester.

"Of course you are. But what do you think about the man?"

"Where is he staying?"

"That's one reason for suspicion. He was evasive when the police asked him. He said he'd been stopping at the hotel temporarily but was looking for more permanent lodgings. At the moment he wasn't sure where they would be. And listen, Hester. You're so — so — oh, I don't know how to say it, but you're sort of an easy mark. You're gullible because you're naturally so kind. It would be just like you to invite him in if he came to the door — "

"At three o'clock in the morning?"

"Now, don't take me wrong. But for heaven's sake just watch out. If the police are puzzled and all the men on the streets around here are telling their wives to be very, very careful then you certainly should be too. The whole thing sounds alarming to me. I was going to tell you this today in any case and this excuse to go to the country was perfect. What would you think of a collie?"

"I — I don't believe so."

"Well, don't let Sandy's behavior influence you. I told you he's just a spoiled brat and you could train another in the way he should go if you got him younger. Even a little dog's bark can scare away a marauder." She leaned closer. "Hester!"

"Yes."

"Don't decide I've gone back to a teen-ager, but you know in spite of the fact I'm scared I think it's sort of exciting to have this strange man roaming our streets at night, looking at the moon. Come on, tell me the truth. How do you feel?"

Hester looked at her friend, and a little more color came into her cheeks. "Well," she said slowly, "of course I'm scared too, but I will admit that life is pretty monotonous for me."

"So anything's a change. Let's have a parfait on it now since we've kept our figures, and then be on our way."

The rest of the trip to the kennels was fortunately uneventful. The estate itself was more beautiful than Hester had imagined. Endless lawns, endless trees and shrubs, a magnificent, spreading Tudor house rising in dignity at the back, a glimpse of a glorious flower garden at the side.

"This can't be the place," Hester exclaimed.

"Oh, yes. Nothing commercial profanes the main residence. We go a little farther and down a dirt road to the kennels themselves. Mrs. Russell is often there herself. I hope she will be today. I'm crazy about her."

"What did they tell the police at the hotel about this — this man?" Hester broke in suddenly.

"Why, they said he had registered under the name of John Justin, New York City, and they felt there was something odd about him. They didn't like his going out every night, for the night watchman would always see that he went into his room again when he got back and it got to be a nuisance."

"Was he — did he behave properly?"

"Oh yes, the room clerk told the police and one of them told Tom that he had elegant manners but somehow they just couldn't figure him out. Why he was here at all and so on, and they would be just as happy when he left."

"I wonder if he means to stay here."

"From the report it sounds like it. That he was even looking for a house."

"Which doesn't seem suspicious."

"Unless," Ginny said, lowering her voice, "he wants a sort of *base* to work from."

"What on earth do you mean — a *base?*"

"Well," Ginny defended, "Tom is nobody's fool and it almost takes dynamite to stir him up but he really doesn't like this man's behavior at all, and he was the one that used the word *base.* He says there's more funny business going on in this country now than we can even read about in the papers. And heaven knows *that's* plenty. I shouldn't have said that about liking a little excitement, for, honestly, I'm frightened."

"So am I," Hester said, "and I believe in the long run monotony isn't so bad."

"Well, here's the turn. Down Sandy. Have his leash ready for me, Hester, will you?"

They could now see ahead of them the row of canine dwellings which many humans would gladly have claimed for their own; also in yips, yaps and barks, ranging in tone from falsetto to bass, the inmates were making their feelings vocal. Sandy at once added his voice to the chorus. Ginny parked the car at the side of the road, held her pet firmly until she had fastened the leash to his collar and then announced her campaign. "Now, I think we'd better get out and walk the rest of the way. I can keep this little devil under better control then. Ah, there's Mrs. Russell herself! What luck! Do you see her beside that farthest kennel to the right? In the lavender suit? She has the most divine sport clothes. Well, we can go on up and I'll introduce you and then I'll walk Sandy back out of the way while you do your looking. But I'll come back when you've decided. You can wave to me."

"But Ginny, I don't think I'm going to get a dog at all — I — "

"You certainly are. After what I just told you? You don't dare be without one. Now come along."

Mrs. Russell was charming, interested in the introductions, in Sandy and in bright generalities, but never once suggesting that she was the seller and Hester a possible buyer. This made for a relaxed atmosphere as Ginny walked the reluctant Sandy back along the road.

"I'm terribly proud of my puppies," Mrs. Russell was saying. "Lots of people, dog lovers, you know, just come to see them with no thought of buying. I'm always quite set up about that. Since you're here would you like to have a look?"

"As easy as that," Hester thought. No pressure, no obligation, and best of all, really, no Ginny to make decisions for her. "We can take a little tour," Mrs. Russell was repeating. "And then perhaps you can watch Sandy while Ginny makes the rounds. Of course you know he didn't come from here. He has a pedigree all right, a mile long, but he is utterly untrained. Oh, well, he's a beauty and they love him so perhaps that's enough. Shall we have a look at the bigger breeds first?"

They saw them — the collies, golden and white and elegantly proud. Hester watched, petted one or two of the older ones, admired the puppies but felt no spark of longing. Perhaps Sandy and his misdemeanors came between her and the plumed beauties. She made it still more clear to Mrs. Russell that she was, in shopping terms, "just looking." And Mrs. Russell assented as though any sale was farthest from her thoughts. She explained carefully, however, what owners could expect from the various dogs, and something of their history. Hester tried to look intelligent and listened carefully.

"So many kennels raise only one kind of dog. To me that would be almost boring. I like all sorts, the different personalities and the amazingly different appearances. You know, a dog is supposed to be the most physiologically pliable of all animals when it comes to breeding. I like to watch those results. Look at that big Newfoundland just being taken out for his exercise. He's a boarder. Enormous, kind, shaggy creature, with more than average intelligence. Put him beside a miniature French poodle! They are both dogs, aren't they? Isn't it fascinating? Isn't it curious? Well, we must get along and I mustn't talk so much."

"But I love it, really," Hester insisted, knowing that the conversation was more interesting to her than the dogs themselves. For as she was introduced to the German shepherds, the sheep dogs, the hunters, the Dalmatians, the bright-eyed squatty dachshunds, the section for the poodles alone and the rest, she found her own eyes growing glazed as she tried to look hard at each canine and keep her expression set in the imitation of a pleased smile.

At last Mrs. Russell announced the tour over, and stood as though uncertain before a pretty little kennel in the shape of a house. "The occupant here is my baby," she said. "I'm a coward for I usually don't show him at all, I'm so afraid someone will want him. He's a cocker spaniel. You know the breed?"

"Not too well," Hester said. "As I'm sure you've recognized, I'm not very knowledgeable about dogs in general."

Mrs. Russell laughed. "I can't play the piano, as I hear you can. Each of us to our specialty. Well, the cocker part of the name came from their English history of hunting woodcocks. The spaniels are all compact little fellows, with silky hair and long droopy ears. Different colors. This one" — she hesitated, and opened the door — "but of course I'll show him to you. He's pure honey."

She moved over to let her guest step in, calling as she did so to the small puppy who was sitting on his haunches, staring out of the window. At her voice he barked joyfully and ran toward her. He was, as she had described, pure honey in color, and as she lifted him up in her arms Hester saw the large melting eyes, the long, silky ears and the ruffles on his short legs which, she recalled now having heard, marked a spaniel as an aristocrat. But all these attributes she merely glanced at and forgot. What happened to her as she stared at the puppy was new, incredible and breathtaking. Emotionally, it was as though a small bolt of lightning had struck her.

"May I hold him?" she found herself asking tremulously.

"But of course. He is a beauty, isn't he? And he's awfully well behaved. Come, Flush, and see the nice lady."

"Flush?"

"Oh, I'm still back with the Brownings as far as poetry goes. I can't make head or tail of most of the modern stuff. So he just had to be Flush!"

Hester pressed the soft, little body to her breast and the puppy, as a token of comfort, cuddled his head under her chin. Something in Hester's heart which had been insensitive, indifferent, even a little hard, now melted and became warmly, almost passionately alive. She held the little dog closer.

"Mrs. Russell," she said in a terror-stricken voice, "you didn't really mean you wouldn't sell him, did you? For I want him more than I can ever remember wanting anything. I *have to have him.* Can't you — ?"

Then Mrs. Russell laughed her pleasant laugh as she leaned over and stroked Flush's head. "I was playing a little game, I confess, for Ginny called me yesterday and told me to be casual and act as though you weren't interested. But about this little fellow, there was some truth to what I said. I would never have parted with him until I saw the buyer was the very right person. And now I see you are, for you're really weeping for fear you lose him. Did you know that? Well, I love him too, and it's very hard to give him up. But there will soon be a new litter. The important thing is that *he* is going to be greatly loved. He is yours, Mrs. Carr. You haven't questioned as to the price."

"Oh, that doesn't matter when I think of having him. We'd better call Ginny, though, and let her know the good news."

"I'll wave my scarf," Mrs. Russell said, putting the action to the word, "and you and I can go into the office for the papers. *You* know, Flush's pedigree and also a diet list and some printed care directions. You can carry him if you want. He will moan if he needs to get down. He's awfully well trained."

When they returned again to the kennels Ginny met them, all smiles which turned to a look of amazement as she saw the small creature in Hester's arms.

"A *cocker!*" she exclaimed. "What use will *that* be as a watchdog?"

Mrs. Russell was the one to answer. "You'd be surprised," she said. "The cockers have a really ferocious-sounding bark and that's all you need, really. Isn't he a beauty, though?"

Ginny agreed but was wistful. "I did so hope you'd pick a collie, Hester, so Sandy would have company. But of course *any* dog's better than none. While I'm hooked on collies, Mrs. Russell, you know I love all kinds, especially yours. Are we ready to go? Sandy's getting impossible to hold."

There were pleasant good-byes while the puppy looked with melting eyes at his former owner and made small efforts to jump.

"Don't let that worry you," Mrs. Russell told Hester.

"He'll respond to you very quickly. See how contented he's been already. And here I just come and go, while you will be with him all the time. "Good-bye, Flushie, dear little dog. I'm glad you're going to have a nice home. I'll just disappear now," she added, "and you hold him close as you go off."

Once in the car, although Hester snuggled him against her breast, she could feel his small frame trembling. He *was* frightened then, and with a dog's uncanny sense knew he was going out into a new and untried world. She did not talk much in answer to Ginny's animated chatter, or even listen to it, but tried to comfort her small charge as well as she could. Once she sat very still and shivered a little even as the puppy.

"Now, as I say," Ginny was remarking, "I certainly don't want to frighten you more than is necessary but Tom thought you should know it all and tell Hattie too. The thing I've kept back is that this man has been seen pausing in front of your house and studying it closely. Bill Hale, who is an architect as you know, says he may just be admiring the *lines,* for it is the best-designed house on the street. But anyway I wish you'd gotten yourself a dog that would soon have some *size.* Well, don't get worked up about it. It may all have a rational explanation. Tom says, though, that he thinks you should ask the police when they patrol our street to pay special attention to your house."

"Of course. Thanks, Ginny. I wish Tom would do it, though. I'll feel a bit like a fool. Do you think he'd speak to them? He's in on it all already. Whatever it is," she added.

"I'll tell him. He's really a lamb about doing things for

other people and he's awfully fond of you, Hester. I wonder I'm not jealous."

Hester laughed. "Thanks for the compliment. And for everything else. I'd never have gone today — I'd never have gotten my precious puppy if it hadn't been for you. I wish I had a strong, decisive character. I wish I hadn't been born under Libra. Now, I'll probably weaken when I have to have it out with Hattie. Here we are, by the way. Wish me well."

"But I thought Hattie *wanted* a dog!"

"Oh, she did but I think her idea was of a Great Dane at the least. You go on, Ginny. Sandy's getting restless. I'll battle it out alone, and thanks a million, darling, for everything."

"And you'd better tell Hattie all I told you," Ginny called softly from the car window. "It's better for her to be on guard, too."

Hester was right. Hattie took one look at the new acquisition and her face registered dismay, disbelief and anger. "You don't mean *that's* what you brought home?" she asked belligerently.

"It's a little cocker spaniel. Isn't he a beauty?"

"Him!" said Hattie. "I could put him in me pocket. What kind of a watchdog will he be?"

"He'll grow even if he never becomes really big. And I'm sure he will bark. It was you that wanted a dog, Hattie."

"I meant a regular one. Not one of these little cocker spaniards."

"*Spaniel,* Hattie, and just feel how soft he is."

Hattie touched the puppy gingerly and he moaned.

"You see. He don't like me. Well, you'd better put him in the bed I've fixed up in the kitchen and then sit down. I've got something to tell you an' you'll wish when you hear it you'd got yourself a proper — Has he got a name?"

"Yes. He's *Flush.*"

Hattie made a small grimace. "That don't sound polite to me. Now Drano would have been a little better. We use them both, but *Flush* — "

"Oh, Hattie, that was the name of a very famous little dog long ago. I'll tell you the story sometime. It doesn't mean what you're thinking. The cockers flush out the birds for the men to shoot. Besides I'm going to call him *Flushie.* Come on. Show me his bed."

It would have accommodated a whole litter comfortably, but at once Hester curved the old blanket into soft cozy little folds; then, after walking him on his new leash a few minutes in the garden, put the puppy in his nest where, exhausted from his trip, he fell at once to sleep.

"Now," said Hattie, figuratively licking her lips, "don't say I never told you so. Don't laugh at me for lockin' up the doors or hearin' sounds in the night. There's something goin' on, Miss Hester, an' we may all be murdered in our beds yet."

"Well now, tell me what it's all about."

Hattie took a step nearer. "Bessie that lives down the street at the Cooks' run up to tell me so we'd sure be warned." Her voice dropped. "There's a strange man walkin' the streets at queer hours like two or three in the morning an' he just keeps lookin' around an' Bessie says the men told the police an' they're patrolling but so far they haven't caught him in a crime but you see he's just bidin' his time, likely, an' who knows where he may strike? An' I was shakin' like a leaf while she told me. She says Mr. Cook's put double locks on all their doors like the ones we have an' he leaves a light on downstairs all night. So there it is, Miss Hester."

Hester's face was serious. "I don't like the situation any more than you do, Hattie. But as a matter of fact I had already heard about it."

"So Mrs. Masters told you."

"She did."

"It just goes to show then that everybody's talking about it because they're scared. An' I want our doors locked early in the evenings, mind, an' you draw down your shades. I've told you about that. You're so sort of trusting. Well, neither of us can be that way anymore. Two lone, lorn women — "

"With a dog."

"Much good that'll do us!" Hattie said darkly and would discuss it no more.

In the main the evening was tranquil. The serving dishes were not steady at dinner showing that Hattie was still nervous but doing her best to control it. The puppy ate his supper, enjoyed apparently a little stroll on the front lawn, allowed himself to be caressed, and then went to sleep in his bed with a low light giving friendly cheer in the kitchen. There was a clock, too, ticking away, as Mrs. Russell had advised, to lend the small newcomer company.

Hester allowed the front door to be closed and locked early, though the weather was mild, played for half an hour on the piano, discussed the day again by phone with Ginny and then, selecting a book, went up to bed by ten o'clock. Once there, however, she found reading difficult so she put out the light and lay thinking. The man. The strange man who went walking along the streets at the hours when other people were normally asleep. So quiet, so innocent seemed his interest in the stars. But suppose his interest was not innocent. Suppose beside him in the shadows lurked an insidious threat to them all or more likely to some one; suppose the darkness of danger walked with the strange man, while the stars watched above, all unheeding?

It was a long time before Hester fell asleep, and when she woke it was through the mists of a drowsy dream in which someone seemed to be moaning. She roused herself enough to listen and then there came plainly the lonely crying of the new puppy. She threw on her robe and hurried down the stairs in the dark until she reached the dimly lighted kitchen. She picked up the small whimpering dog and snuggled him to her breast. At once the sounds stopped as he nestled more closely to her. He was so little, so soft and dear and all her own. She couldn't leave him here. She would take him up to her bedroom.

She wrapped him in his blanket and started out toward the front stairs. How quiet a house could be at three in the morning, as the tall clock noted the hour. Suddenly, breaking the stillness, Hester heard the sound of footsteps on the pavement outside. She listened. They came on, slowly, steadily. With a quick movement in keeping with her heartbeat she moved to the narrow panel at the side of the front door, and watched. A man came deliberately along the sidewalk, looking now at the houses, now up at the stars. The growing moonlight he had mentioned a few nights ago to the police was now a spreading white. In the midst of it he was now moving directly in front of her house. Hester all but stopped breathing and leaned against the wall behind her. When she could make a sound it was like a little trembling breath.

"It can't be," she whispered. "Oh, it *can't be!*"

But in her heart she knew that it was.

CHAPTER TWO

THE DIGNIFIED LITTLE SUBURB of Westbrook, where men in white shirts took the wheezy train each morning to reach their work in the city, had not grown with the rapidity of other towns along the line. For one reason, it lay almost at the end of the branch road so the commuters' trip was a longer one than most.

"And so what?" Tom Masters was wont to say. "By the time I've read the paper and worked the puzzle I'm there, so what's wrong with that? Besides, look at the advantages we have in Westbrook."

And this, indeed, was true. There were advantages for those who could appreciate them. There was no unseemly encroachment of brash new developments with modern angles set at variance with the solid colonial or English-type architecture of which the town was largely composed. Rather, an unobtrusive elegance pervaded the streets. Even the shopping center, still referred to as "The Village" by the older residents, or "The Row" by the younger, gave the impression of calm, rather than commercial hurry. The families living in Westbrook seemed to stop with three children at the most, so the schools were not overcrowded and were good. There was a modest country club and golf course to the north of the town with small pleasant hills cradling it on the east and south. But the second reason why many prospective buyers studied vacant lots here and there in Westbrook and then told the real estate agent they believed they would look further at other communities, lay a little to the west. For here was another town quite, quite different. It was shabby with most of its nondescript houses needing paint, occasional ramshackle stables, reminiscent of horse and buggy days, still standing, or rather, leaning precariously, along the back alleys. There was a general store of sorts, shabby also, usually with a few men sitting lazily on the steps chewing tobacco. Instead of neat flower gardens kept by professionals, there were, in the small town, patches of vegetables, often at the front, with boards laid between the beet or onion rows. Many of the women were seen only at a distance by the ladies of Westbrook, but it was reported that summer washings were done in big tubs in the backyards. Children abounded. There was evidently no limitation of families and since the town was over the Westbrook township line it had its own school: a dingy, two-story brick.

The name of the place was Sackville and it had been there long, long before suburbia arrived, family by family, to become a neighbor. Over the years, new young trees had grown to spreading ones, concealing much of the distant and unsightly view from the eyes of the citizens of Westbrook. Daily custom had also played its part. There was, too, a grudging admission that Sackville would be missed if it should one day be suddenly swallowed up, for in it dwelt the carpenter, the tinner, the mason, the plumber, the men of all work whose apprenticeship had been served in the school of hard necessity; and, also, certain women who would "oblige" at house-cleaning time for general day work or to clean up after large parties. Sackville then, even though useful, was a blot upon the beauty of the landscape, but refused, despite all efforts of real estate brokers and private buyers, to remove itself. It liked to be just where it was. Where it had always been, there it intended to remain.

On the morning after Hester's troubled night, both she and the little dog slept late. Hattie finally went up to the bedroom and gently pushed open the door. At once there was movement at the foot of the bed and Hattie said, "Well, I never!" Hester opened her eyes, sat up suddenly and, without waiting, began upon her defense.

"Well, you see, I wakened in the night to the most pitiful little cries — I think it was a mistake to leave him there all by himself — so I slipped down and brought him up here with me and he cuddled down and went right to sleep. And I *like* to have him here, so don't say a word."

Hattie sniffed. "Everyone to her taste. Mine wouldn't be sleeping with a dog. But what I wanted to tell you was that Bill Hoover's down on the back porch waiting to saw off that dead cherry-tree limb that's been makin' all the racket when the wind blows. You'd better get down an' tell him where to cut. He's in no hurry, you can be sure. I'll give him some coffee. And hadn't I better take this cocker spaniard down an' give him a little run in the yard?"

"Oh, please, Hattie, but he's a *spaniel,* not a Spaniard."

"Well, whatever he is, he ain't much of a lookin' dog to me!"

She gathered him up gently, however, and Hester had a feeling that affection would soon follow. As to her coming encounter with Bill Hoover, she felt extreme distaste. While most of the workmen who came from Sackville, to make the houses of Westbrook more secure in various ways, were dirty, unshaven and often tattered of shirt and trousers, they were, as a rule, respectful and rather silent. Not so Bill Hoover. He had what Hester to herself called "a wicked eye," and his conversation flowed freely if anyone would listen; when he paused now and then it was to give to the woman within reach a crooked smirk, which perhaps might better be called a *leer.*

"I wouldn't trust him 'round a stump," was Hattie's pronouncement. "He looks like a lecherous old jailbird to me. Mind, I'll be in the kitchen when you're talkin' to him."

Hester found her guest placidly contemplating the garden with his empty cup beside him.

"Mornin', Missus Carr. Nice little pup you got there. Want to sell him?"

"No," Hester said shortly, "I don't. Now about this cherry limb, Bill, I'll tell you just where I want it cut. Did you bring your saw?"

Bill slapped his thigh. "Now that's a good one on me. 'Come up and saw off a tree limb, Bill?' you says, an' here I come without my saw. Come on. There'll mebbe be one in the garridge."

"We can hope so," Hester answered, a faint irony in her

voice, since her tools, so carefully kept by Walter, had a way of disappearing now after Sackville workmen had used them. This time a saw was found and Bill, after the appearance of back-breaking labor, finally mounted on a low ladder, dismembered the limb and settled himself again on the porch to recuperate. Hattie appeared at once at the kitchen door.

"Well, Bill, I judge when you get that limb drug away an' the saw put in place, we might owe you about five dollars. It's too much, but I will say that limb was a nuisance, makin' noise and wakin' me up nights. Here's a sandwich for you an' I'll bring you a cup of coffee, Mrs. Carr. You might as well have it here where it's sunny and see that everything's put to rights before he leaves. Then you can have your breakfast in peace. I'll feed the dog."

"Awful nice little animal, that," Bill remarked as he chewed his sandwich with relish. "Me, I was allays for hound dogs myself till this last one. He took turrible sick an' died on me an' seems like I can't stomach another hound. Guess I set too much store by this one. I called him Bill Junior 'cause I allays wanted a boy and my wife never gave me nothin' but girls, *seven* of 'em. She just done it for spite."

"Why Bill, you ought to be ashamed. She couldn't help having girls!"

"You don't understand how ornery my wife is," he answered and then added, "God knows I done *my* part all right."

"About the saw," Hester said hastily, "I would like you to use one of those old cloths in the garage and shine it up nicely before you put it in the drawer where it's always kept."

"Sure, sure. Now that little dog you got, if you ever want to dispose of it — might get to be too much trouble or something — you just let me know an' I'll take it off your hands and I'll work it out. No matter what you paid for it, I'll work it out, if it takes me a year, so I will. I've took kind of a fancy to that pup."

Hester laughed. "How can I make you understand, Bill? Nothing could buy my little dog. You just told me how you felt about your Bill Junior. Well, I'm going to be just that way about Flushie."

"*Flushie?* Bitch, is it?"

"He is a male," Hester said with dignity.

"Name sounds sort of female to me. Well, I guess I better get goin' on my work. Wouldn't be surprised if I sprained my back on that ladder. Reachin' and all. Miss Hattie, she hain't no mercy on workmen, I allays say. Now you're different, Missus Carr. You're a reg'lar lady an' Mr. Carr was openhanded, that he was."

He started to cross the lawn and then came back. He put one dirty, horny hand at the side of his mouth to indicate secrecy.

"Them noises Miss Hattie was talkin' about, do you think they was just this old limb creakin'?"

"Certainly. What else would they be? When the wind stopped they stopped."

"I don't know whether I'd ought to say this, you an' Miss Hattie livin' alone an' all, but *there's talk goin' 'round.*"

"What about?" Hester tried to make her tone casual.

"Well, you know, there's women in Sackville come up here betimes to wash an' clean an' such for some of the ladies an' they get the news, specially when the kitchen door's left open. Seems there's a man keeps walkin' round at night at sort of funny hours an' once anyway, he was in Sackville! Belle Jackson was up 'bout three o'clock heatin' milk for her kid — he's always been puny — an' she heard steps an' looked out the window an' there he was, walkin' past just like the ladies up here had said. An' she set up an hour just watchin' every turn he took till he started back to Westbrook."

"It's a free country," Hester tried to say calmly. "Anyone can take a walk."

"Well," Bill said belligerently, "these men up here wear pants with creases in 'em an' white shirts, but us men in Sackville don't wear no kid gloves. I'm tellin' you, if he ain't up to no good, this strange fellah, we'll take care of him."

He had gone to the garage before Hester could think of an appropriate reply. When he had finished the last small chores, however, he came back to the porch as she was rising. He had an odd look in his eye. Mingled with his usual leer at the sight of feminine beauty, there was also a certain shrewdness.

"Funny thing, Belle Jackson said, was that he seemed to know his way 'round," and with this he ambled off.

Hester walked slowly across the porch trying to shake off certain disturbing thoughts which seemed like the fragmentations of a dream. Then she laughed. If anyone could make a queer story sound more queer, it would be Bill.

Know his way 'round, indeed. There was only one real street in Sackville with a spattering of shantylike houses and a few stables slanting off from it at intervals. And as to her own reactions to the quiet pedestrian last night, she felt now, in the bright reality of day, that her guess had been impulsive and ridiculous. She would certainly wait until she had more proof, if there could be such a thing.

She opened the door and almost stepped upon the small form waiting there. She gathered him into her arms with little crooning sounds she had never known she could make. He was so silky, so tenderly soft. His nose, she discovered, was pure velvet, nothing like Sandy's, for instance.

"And look, Hattie, what a strong, square little chest he has, with an incipient white shirt-front ruffle, actually, oh, I love him!"

"Well now, don't get carried away. Come an' eat your breakfast an' use some common sense. He seems quiet enough, so maybe he'll be easy to manage. That's one thing I'll say for him. Put him down now an' wash your hands."

Hester giggled, thinking that while Walter would never have understood nor approved the feeling, Hattie's bossiness gave her mistress a soothing sense of childlike security.

Breakfast, usually a rather dull meal, took on exciting novelty that morning, for Flushie sat as close to Hester as was possible, watching her with melting eyes and with hopeful and almost audible swallowings as the pungent odors of bacon and scrambled eggs rose from one platter and of hot muffins from another. When Hattie had left the room, Hester spoke aloud, firmly. "This is what I must never do," she quoted. Then, with a delicious sense of guilt, she offered her pet first a bit of bacon, then, after its instantaneous disappearance, a small segment of muffin. Flushie edged closer, wagging his abbreviated tail and licking his lips.

"The kennels were never like this, were they, doggie, my lad," Hester said laughing. It struck her suddenly how often she had laughed that morning. A strange, unaccustomed delight, certainly in sharp contrast to the recent dinner when the tears had all but dropped into her soup. "But we must show great restraint in this matter, Flushie," she added.

"I say you'd better show restraint," Hattie echoed as she came in with fresh coffee. "If you're not careful, you'll clear lose your head over this dog. After all, you must mind, he's just an animal. Of course," she added, leaning on Walter's chair, "I have to say he's a well-behaved little critter. Not like that Sandy. I wanted a collie bad enough, but at least we could have trained him. There's a car comin' in now. It's Miss Ginny, all right, but she's by herself, that's a blessing. We don't want no ruckus between dogs here. Would you like coffee for the two of you on the porch?"

"Yes, Hattie. That would be fine. I'll go and meet Mrs. Masters."

Ginny was already on the porch when Hester reached it. She was eager-eyed, flushed and evidently bursting with news.

"Coffee! Hattie, you're inspired. I only had three cups this morning for I had to hurry so. Oh, this is absolute heaven. I left Sandy wailing, but I had no time to bother with him. How's the pup doing?"

"He's perfect and you might say my emotions have become definitely involved." Hester laughed.

"You'll get worse and worse. That's the way it goes. But listen, I haven't got long to stay and I have the most tremendous news! Guess what happened! Last night, when Tom got on the train it was packed. Someone sat down beside him and it was *The Man.*"

"No!"

"Yes, and Tom said before he knew it they were talking and he liked this Mr. Justin, for that's his name, tremendously. Tom sort of felt around for clues and Mr. Justin was completely open and above board. He said he supposed someone besides the police was suspicious of his nighttime rambling! 'I was afraid I'd get caught at that,' he said. Tom told him we had all suspected the worst, but had finally settled on burglary and Mr. Justin just laughed and laughed."

"Well, what explanation *did* he give?" Hester asked, a slight edge in her voice.

"Why, bless you, he's a professor and he's taking his sabbatical and wanted a nice quiet place to study and do some writing, so he's rented that darling little cottage at the end of Canterbury Row, the one everyone is so crazy about, only it's too small for a family. But Mr. Justin says it's just right for him. Aren't you excited, Hester?"

"Why, not particularly. I feel rather deflated. I was all built up for larceny or murder and here we have only a sedate college professor on our hands. But why the walks, even so? Did he explain them?"

"Of course, didn't I tell you? He likes to work until about three in the morning, then he's tired and he has a drink of hot milk — "

"Oh, he *is* wild!" Hester murmured.

"Now don't be sarcastic. Tom and I do that ourselves sometimes when we can't sleep. Then he takes a walk under the stars and is completely relaxed. He said if he was a family man he couldn't keep such queer hours, so he must be a bachelor!" Ginny ended triumphantly. "And here, I think, is the really amazing part of the whole thing. Tom is always slow to make new friendships, but he's simply fallen for Mr. Justin. He says he has charm and he thinks we should invite him to dinner. So the plan is for us to call at once and ask him for next Saturday night. You'll come, Hester, won't you?"

Hester hesitated a moment and then gave her bright smile. "Of course I'll come. Do you think I would miss seeing the mystery man in person? Besides, I love your parties."

"That's good," Ginny said, "but I know you only too well. You've got an 'if' or a 'but' somewhere in your mind, so come out with it."

"Well, I feel just a little as though I had put a jigsaw puzzle together and found one piece missing. I know it's silly and after I meet Mr. Justin I'll probably be completely satisfied. The fact that Tom likes him goes a long way with me. Come on, let's find Flushie."

The dog was sitting at the screen door peering sadly through at his mistress who picked him up immediately.

"I can never thank you enough for what you did, Ginny. I may be an unmitigated fool, but I feel that life has suddenly taken on *meaning,* as they say."

"How's Hattie liking him?"

Hester looked to right and left. "She's funny. Outwardly she pretends he's a nuisance, but I've caught her petting him when she thought I wasn't near and I swear, once I heard her call him Baby!"

Ginny laughed. "Give her time. She'll be worse than you. Oh, he is a darling! Now I must run and spread the news. I'm really a little disappointed, though, at the way you took it. I thought you'd be so relieved and excited too." At the steps she turned suddenly. "Why should you say there's a piece missing out of the puzzle?"

"I don't know. That idea just popped into my head. Probably crazy. Do we all dress Saturday night?"

"Oh, not the men. I don't want it to seem stiff. We gals can wear cocktail dresses and that will jazz it up enough. Wear that blue silk, Hester, you look like an angel in that. And bring your brains along. I haven't many."

Hester followed her to the car. "Where does he teach?"

"He didn't volunteer and Tom didn't like to ask him. But you know what an Anglophile Tom is. He has to tell everyone about our trip to England last summer, so he asked Mr. Justin if he'd ever been to Oxford. And Tom said Mr. Justin sort of smiled and said he had spent some time studying there as a young man."

"Rhodes Scholar," Hester half whispered.

"Now what made you think of that?" Ginny asked, amused. "For that was just what Tom said when he told me about it. He says Mr. Justin is very modest and reticent, but he did admit to being there three years when Tom pressed him. Well, if that's the case, I think you ought to be satisfied *now*. And wear the blue dress," she called as she started the car, "for he's evidently a bachelor."

Hester went back into the house again where Hattie spoke up promptly.

"She acted like she's got a bee in her bonnet again. What is it this time?"

Hester told her briefly what Mr. Masters had discovered. Hattie's shrewd eyes narrowed.

"A pretty howdy-do," she said, then adding for emphasis, "A likely story! Couldn't that man make up anything if he's smart an' tell it like it's the truth? Who's to know the difference? Is that all she told you?"

"No," Hester said, determined to get it over with. "Mr. and Mrs. Masters are going to call on him and invite him to dinner Saturday night with a few very carefully selected guests to sort of — "

"Size him up," said Hattie.

"Welcome him to the community!" Hester finished.

"Well, they say there's one born every minute, but I'm tellin' you it's oftener than that in Westbrook. An' do speak to Miss Ginny about countin' her silver before the party. You can't be too careful. And listen, Miss Hester, I got a little more news myself today."

"Oh, what?"

"Belle Hoover stopped in on her way up to Mrs. Forbes' to clean. She often drops in for a cup of coffee, poor soul, an' she told me about seein' the man on the Sackville street *in the wee hours of the night,* as the sayin' goes, an' he jouked into that little alley next to Windy Hays' tin shop an' it hurries anybody livin' there even to see that in the dark. Belle says it give her a turn sort of, but she thinks he could have heard a dog yappin' or something an' just wanted to get out of the way."

"That could very likely be the reason."

"Still an' all, Belle says she's sort of scared and the men say they'll just take him apart if he ever does anything he oughtn't to in Sackville."

"Nonsense! He's a gentleman. A professor in a college. He's writing a book and he works at night. When he gets tired he takes these walks to relax him. That's all there is to it."

"Humph!" said Hattie. "Sounds fine. As for me, I'll lock the doors."

In the rich August sunshine, Hester took Flushie for a stroll along the avenue that ran at right angles to her own street, then when she got back, sat down in the backyard under the maple, that was still green and bright with summer. She knew that she must, insofar as possible, reconstruct the memory that haunted her now like a ghost that would not be laid. And as she dropped inhibitions with the clouds of the years, everything came back with amazing clarity.

It had happened on shipboard during the deliriously happy trip she had taken with her mother just before sorrows too great for her young heart had fallen upon her. It had been the last night out, with all sorts of gaiety, dancing and music. Her mother felt tired and went to her cabin, but Hester had gone out to the deck and leaned upon the rail transported by the sight of the full moon upon the quiet sea.

Suddenly she was aware of a young man, somewhat older than she, standing beside her looking keenly at her face which was turned toward the moonlight. He laughed, a pleasant, winning laugh.

"Now isn't it remarkable," he began, "that in this vale of tears two happy people such as you and I should meet? For somehow I feel you are happy, aren't you?"

"Oh yes!" Hester had answered, as though the question was the most natural in the world. "It's my first trip abroad, and if my mother keeps well we'll be staying some time in Paris, so that I can study."

"What?" he asked eagerly.

"Oh, *music!*" She laid an involuntary hand on her heart. "I feel it so. I love it so. But tell me why *you* are so happy."

He looked about him. They were alone for the few moments as though upon a little oasis of humanity. "I'll tell you if it doesn't sound like bragging. I'm so thrilled and excited, it will be a relief to tell it right out to you and the moon. I've been selected as a Rhodes Scholar and I'm going to Oxford to study for three years and I can't believe it. It's incredible *for me.* It's a miracle! And I want to go shouting it to everyone I meet. But I've really been most circumspect until I saw you standing here alone smiling at the moon. Then I couldn't resist telling you. For you *were* smiling," he added.

"I'm so glad you did, for I'm fairly bursting with joy myself and I don't believe I realized it until I saw you and felt I could say it all out loud!"

"Do you believe in the so-called Emotional Scales?" he asked abruptly. "That life strikes a balance. So much sorrow or pain on one side, an equal amount of pleasure and happiness on the other? Do you believe that?"

"I never even heard of it."

"Then let's forget it." He added in a lower tone, "I've had enough trouble on one scale to balance my feelings now. Oh, let's just enjoy happiness tonight. It's an active ingredient, you know."

They had gone on, she remembered, touching lightly on this and that until at last he had quoted softly:

> The sea is calm tonight.
> The tide is full, the moon lies fair

"Please don't finish," she begged. "You know you'll run right into the line about the eternal note of sadness. We don't want that, do we?"

"Heavens, no! How could I have slipped up on it? Good old 'Dover Beach.' We'll give it a miss. But how wonderful we like the same poetry! We could probably talk all night and never run out of subject matter. I'm afraid, though, I've kept you too late as it is and your mother will be anxious. Let's just say good-bye without introducing ourselves. It would break something fragile and lovely to hear ordinary names and places. Let's just be ships that pass in the night so nothing will mar the memory of this perfect little happy time. Are you satisfied?"

"Yes," she had answered, "names sometimes break a spell."

"I do know your cabin number, for I once had a brief glimpse of you going in. I really belong down below, but dinner clothes have helped me get by up here now and then. Before we part, could you play the Moonlight Sonata? It may seem to you a schoolgirlish piece, but it just suits the mood of the scene now. Do you know it? The little music room there is deserted at the moment."

"Of course," she answered quickly. She knew it from memory and, sitting in the shadow, she played. He stood in the doorway, his face lighted from the pale shine of the moon and the deck lanterns. When she had finished, he was gone.

She went to her cabin, hugging to her heart the strange and, to her, romantic incident. In the morning a note addressed only to "Cabin 415" was brought to her by a steward. It read:

> *Dear little ship that passed*
> *in the night. Let's always*
> *be happy, shall we?*
> *Thank you so much for the Sonata.*

It was signed *The Other Ship.*

This card she laid carefully away at the time with other small souvenirs of the trip: the program of the big concert; the menu of the dinner at the captain's table; a small sketch an artist had done of her; even the tag on her deck chair — all sorts of tiny mementos of the wonderful voyage. She was very young. Her heart was very tender, very full of hope and anticipation, eager for each smallest interlude of joy.

They would not of course, she knew, disembark at the same place. She and her mother would be going on to Cherbourg. She had not seen him again. She thought of him often for the first week or so, remembering his face as it had stood out clearly in the soft light. Her own as they talked, and certainly as she played the Sonata, had been rather in the shadow. Sometimes she took out the little card, read it and smiled, then put it away again with her "keepsakes."

But then came her mother's illness, the sudden return

home, sorrow upon sorrow as the year passed. There came also her removal to Aunt Cissie's home and the advent of Walter and his steady attentions. It was as she was clearing out the drawers and closets of her old room that she swept away all the girlish relics and souvenirs of the past, her tears falling, not for the pictures, cards and oddments themselves, but for the young and happy girl she had once been. On her wedding day, she felt, as Walter kept repeating, that she was indeed beginning a new life. And now, after all the years, once again out of the moonlight, a face! Or could it really be?

The evening of the dinner party was pleasantly warm with a little west wind blowing. Hester wore the blue dress, a thin brocade with a wide neck and short cap sleeves. It fell in straight and graceful elegance almost to her knees. She flushed as she looked at herself. In spite of the tiny inevitable marks of time which would keep her from being mistaken for a young girl, her cheeks were soft, her throat firm, her body still slender. She knew she was a very pretty woman and the fact that this thought had crossed her own mind and might cross those of others tonight gave her a feeling of guilt or, rather, a sort of remorse, that Walter was not there to see and know and be proud of her.

She was ready early, so she started downstairs as usual to be inspected by Hattie. "Come, my little sweet," she said to Flushie, who never needed the invitation. Indeed, with incredible dexterity, he managed to stay beside her wherever she was. Even in the mornings on the way to her bath, he somehow insinuated himself through the door and then stood with his front paws on the edge of the tub watching with interest and, it would seem, admiration as she splashed gently in the perfumed water. And while at times she took herself strongly to task for the strength of her emotions toward Flushie, she always ended by drawing him close as though something long wished for and denied her was now her own.

Hattie examined the costume of her mistress, picked an imaginary thread therefrom, checked the hook and eye at the top of the zipper and said, "Well, I guess you'll do. You're not walkin', are you?"

"I could, easily enough. Indeed, I'd like to, but Mr. Masters insisted on coming around for me. So silly, when it's only two streets over."

"Not a bit," said Hattie. "I don't like to see you stravagin' around alone when queer people are runnin' loose."

Hester laughed and Flushie, at the sound, wagged his short tail violently. "Don't you know," she went on, "this dinner party is to explain away all mysteries?"

There was the sound of a car door and a step on the walk. Flushie moved closer with something like despair in his liquid eyes. "He knows I'm leaving," Hester said. "Be good to him, Hattie."

"I'll take him on the back porch an' feed him an' pet him up a little," was the surprising answer.

As Hester stepped forward to meet him, Tom whistled and Flushie pricked up his ears.

"You mustn't do that, Tom," Hester laughed. "It's not *seemly*, as the older generation would say and besides, you excite my dog. Good boy, Flushie," she added, stooping to drop a kiss on his satin head. "You go along with Hattie and I'll be back before long. Good, good little dog."

"Some lucky pup, I'd say." Tom grinned. "Well, we'd better start. Ginny's in very high feather and has definitely set out to impress Mr. Justin, with all the resources she owns or can borrow. I suppose she's filled you in on all the main points?"

"Oh yes," Hester said as she got into the car, "but I can stand a few more details."

"It's a funny thing," Tom went on, "I was really the leader of all the hue and cry against the strange night walker. I thought it was queer and might be dangerous — until this fellow sat down in the seat beside me with his briefcase. He'd been up at the New York library, he said. Well, when he smiled and sort of shyly introduced himself, I just fell for him, hook, line and sinker. And I don't fall easily," he added. "He said he'd seen me get on the train that morning, so he knew I lived in Westbrook."

"And where does he teach?"

"A college called Darlington Institute, chiefly, I gathered, for graduate students."

"It seems to me he told you a good deal upon short acquaintance."

"Not really," said Tom. "I asked some questions and then when he heard about the rumors, he was quite amused and said he had better clear himself at once. That's how it came about. I'd say he's naturally reticent."

"Well, I'll wait to form my opinion," Hester said, smiling. "Here we are. Why, the guests are coming along the street in *hordes.*"

"Of course. Nothing as exciting as this has happened in

Westbrook for ages. I think we're to be twelve at table. Well, here we go."

The guest of honor was already there, chatting with Ginny in the wide hall. Tom stepped beside her and introduced Hester who felt her color rising. The face, though older, came back to her clearly in memory.

"Mrs. Carr?" he was saying as he bowed slightly over her hand. "I have a strange feeling that we have met before. Could I be right?"

"The world is so wide," Hester answered with a nervous little tremor in her voice.

"That's true," the man said, laughing. "I have two friends who met after years on the back of two camels standing side by side in Egypt."

More guests were coming just then and the greetings were over. But when they were all seated at last at the dinner table, a pleasant relaxation seemed to fall on everyone. There was actual merriment as, with Tom's leading questions and the stranger's answers, the mysteries were explained away.

"I know it must have looked queer," the latter said ruefully, "but I got started on a book that has me baffled most of the time. I've always worked best at night and when I get to feeling completely blocked, I go out and take a walk. That's all there is to it."

"Now, here's the payoff," said Tom. "Our officers are going to be frightfully disappointed at having all their suspicions melt under their eyes. But they are sure to cling to one. That is, that you carried one hand in your pocket and they were waiting, you see, for a gun to pop out."

Everyone laughed except the guest of honor. For a second he looked embarrassed and there was a distinct holding of breaths.

"I feel silly, that's all," he said at last, "because it sounds so childish. I was in a car accident once and got off very luckily except for a hand injury. While it was bandaged I carried it in my pocket to save questions and later I guess it became a habit of sorts. Two fingers stayed a bit stiff and I think I just 'cosseted' them as the old expression goes. I'm afraid this will be a blow to your policemen. What a disappointment I'm turning out to be all around."

It was a gay dinner. Something in the stranger's keen mind and contagious wit sent ripples of bright conversation around the table. As she listened and took her part, Hester studied her friends and wondered what the stranger would think of them. Even to her, who had a fondness for them all, they seemed a bit smug, a bit settled into the pleasant, even grooves of suburbia. The men, off to their morning trains to read the news and do the puzzles and then pursue their daily routine. But was this not life? What else could they do but provide for their families according to their training? And the women? Here she came in herself. There was some church work for most of them, some trips to the city to plays or concerts and then, filling in all the extra time — afternoons with each other and evenings with the men — bridge. This was Westbrook. This perhaps, was suburbia everywhere.

She realized suddenly that she had been sitting silent and that the stranger was speaking to her, for Ginny had insisted upon placing her at Tom's right with the stranger next to her.

"Do forgive me," she said. "I thought you were quite engaged with Helen Drew."

"I was," he said, "but I think it's time to turn the table. I still have the queer feeling I've met you somewhere before, but whether or not, I hope to see you again soon and hear what philosophy was going through your head just now. Do you live near here?"

"Yes, just two streets over."

"May I walk you home? I haven't a car as yet."

"Yes. Thank you. I'd like the walk. But I wasn't dealing in philosophy just now. I was wondering how a group such as ours here in Westbrook would seem to a man from a different world, meaning you," she added, smiling.

He looked startled for a minute as though she had surprised him in his own thoughts and then spoke lightly. "First and most of all, friendly. You can see how this quality would appeal to a lonely man. It wouldn't occur to me to analyze further. At least, not tonight," he added. "Anyway, our hostess is rising. Oh, and thank you for giving me immunity on my walk tonight."

They laughed together and repaired with the others to the living room. It had been learned that Mr. Justin, as he said, could play bridge after a fashion if he had to, but with congenial friends would rather talk, so the guests regrouped and conversation began again. When Ginny finally asked Hester to play the piano, the latter rose without protest.

"It's shameless of me always to agree so willingly but, you see, it's much more exciting to play for other people than just for myself. Can you suggest a few things you'd like?"

As she ran over favorite after favorite, Mr. Justin spoke at last. "Do you know the Moonlight Sonata? I've always been fond of it."

Hester looked up once and saw him listening with a half-puzzled face as though in an attempt at recall. Tom pleaded for songs before she left the piano and the men rose eagerly to stand close for harmonizing — a usual ending to the dinner parties.

"Come on, Justin," Tom invited. "Come and join us even if you don't sing."

But they all soon found he did, with a rich, steady bass. When they started one piece with which he was not familiar, he moved closer where he could see the music and then sang on without missing a note. Hester turned to him at once.

"Why, you read!" she said in surprise.

"Oh, I used to play the fiddle a little before I got a couple of stiff fingers. No virtuoso." He smiled.

When the singing was over there were suggestions that it was long past time to go home, followed by very eloquent thanks for the evening and especially by good wishes to their new neighbor.

"Wait. I'll run you home, Hester," Tom said.

"Oh, it's right on my way," Henry Dunn insisted.

But the stranger spoke up strongly. "Please," he said. "Mrs. Carr has agreed to let me walk her home, thus making me a reputable character if any gentlemen of the law see me with her. Agreed?"

There was much laughter and many witty remarks as Justin and Hester said their good-byes and strolled off up the street. They didn't speak at once, conscious of Ginny and Tom still in the doorway. When they had passed out of earshot, the man said earnestly, "I loved your playing tonight. You must have studied a great deal."

"As much as I could," she answered. "But you! I do not want to sympathize with you about losing touch with your violin, for I have a feeling you'll still get it back."

"I'm afraid not now. It's been over five years. I feel worse than ever when I put it to the test, so I don't do it anymore."

"That's not right," Hester said quickly. "Never give up on it. I'll tell you what we could do. Did you bring your violin with you?"

"Oh yes. It's my friend. I'd never leave it behind."

"Good. Then couldn't you bring it down some evening and let me play some simple thing and you try again no matter how it sounded at first? Would you do that? I'll throw in one of Hattie's good dinners to tempt you," she added laughing.

"I don't need further temptation, Mrs. Carr," he said quietly. "Your kindness is quite enough. But yes, if you can stand the sounds, I'll be only too happy to try. For your sake," he added.

"We'll set a night then. When I think of what my music means to me, I'm wild with delight over the possibility of bringing yours back to you. What about next Tuesday evening with dinner at seven?"

"Wonderful! But please don't be disappointed if nothing happens. Of course, an accompaniment would help. All my attempts were in my room alone and the hopeless, unrelieved sounds just sent me into despair. Now you see, I'll have the visit with you to think of and your own music to enjoy, so I may not be so tense and ready to give up right away."

They chatted on as they walked, of music, of the party just over, of the house Mr. Justin had bought and the architecture of Hester's.

"I stood outside your house one night admiring its lines. It's beautifully proportioned. Westbrook has definite charm."

"What you just said gives me courage to ask you one more question, though I'm afraid you have already been plied with too many tonight. But this is all my own. You are writing a book and wanted a quiet place to work and spend your sabbatical. Just why did you happen to choose Westbrook?"

For long seconds he did not answer and Hester, sensitively embarrassed, spoke first.

"Oh, please consider that unsaid. It bordered on the personal and so was really rude. Do forgive me."

"There is certainly nothing to forgive. It was a most natural question. I only hope you'll excuse me if I don't seem to answer it fully. This much I can say: I came to Westbrook in the hope of paying a long-standing debt."

CHAPTER THREE

OH, THE BEAUTY of those September days! No leaf changed color as the month advanced; no haze began to cloud the hills; no early blight fell upon the garden. It was still summer although the calendar page had turned, and gently as the days followed each other, the friendship between Hester and John Justin developed.

He had come that first night appointed, to dinner, making friends without effort, it seemed, with both Hattie and Flush. The former, nose in air, had shown a stiff and suspicious attitude at the beginning. Near the end of the meal, when Mr. Justin had praised her lemon pie with touching sincerity, she relaxed and, pausing behind Walter's chair, admitted that the meringue had been a bit too brown.

"I'm really a very ordinary and innocent sort of man," he

said with a friendly smile as he helped her put out the candles. "You don't have to worry about your locks anymore at night."

"Well, that's a comfort anyway," Hattie remarked and Hester knew that he had won the day.

Flushie took to his new friend more slowly. He followed and sat close to Hester but, little by little, moved over to the stranger and sniffed appreciatively. Finally he lay down at his feet. Justin made no effort at first to touch him, but after a time he bent over and stroked his head gently and Flushie licked his hand.

"Two conquests in one evening!" Hester said, laughing. "You do well. Seriously, though, I'm glad Hattie, especially, has accepted you. I was sure Flushie would, but Hattie's prejudices run very deep. Well, now we can be comfortable about her."

"That pie would melt any male heart of stone! When will you play for me?"

"At once, if you wish." She went to the piano and decided, now that they were alone, to see if remembrance of things past would rise again. She had played only a few minutes when he sprang from his chair, dislodging Flushie as he did so. He was at the piano in a bound, facing her.

"But we *have* met! I was sure of it and I could still be mistaken but I don't think so. Didn't we stand together talking once at the deck rail on a moonlit night years ago when we were young? Didn't we?"

She looked up, smiling. "Yes, we did. I remembered too."

"But what a clod I've been. I was haunted by some sort

of disjointed memory which I couldn't put together. And you didn't help me, you know," he added.

"I thought I'd better be sure too."

He reached out both hands and she put hers in them. "But now, we both remember! It's amazing! It's miraculous! That I should come here as a stranger and find an old friend!" He was exuberant.

"Yes, I think it's rather incredible too. Do you remember what we talked about that night? I think we were only together a short time."

"I thought you were so young and the hour was late and I was afraid your mother would be worried. Oh, we talked about *happiness,* I do remember that."

"You said, 'Let's always be happy!' "

"What a foolish thing."

"Yes, but it seemed to fit the night. And we decided not to introduce ourselves for fear" — she laughed — "it would break a spell or something."

"Oh, that comes back to me. And my asking you to play. Then I slipped off, didn't I? I was out of bounds there anyway. Oh, let's sit down and be comfortable and think it all over, shall we? I'm terribly excited!"

They sat on the sofa with Flushie between them and in tiny bits and pieces reconstructed much of their young conversation. It was Hester who remembered most.

"You sent a little card to my stateroom the next morning. You said you had seen me go in and remembered the number."

"I did? What did it say?"

"I'm afraid it's long been lost, but I remember you called

me the little ship that passed in the night and signed yourself *The Other Ship*! I thought it was terribly romantic and kept it with my other souvenirs for quite some time until they all had to be disposed of. But it *was* sweet, wasn't it?"

"Yes," he said gravely, "I think it was. And why don't we stop there. I went to England, you to France, and sometime again we can go on with the story. I would rather like to leave it there now, as we stopped once before. Shall we?"

"Yes, we mustn't overdo it. Besides, my good sir, we have work to do."

"You can't mean after this you will listen to my horrible squeaks?"

"More than ever now, for we're friends. Get your fiddle and let's begin."

The first attempt was bad, the second was worse and Justin was turning to put the violin in its case when Hester stopped him.

"How can you possibly give up now? Come on, try again. I'll make the accompaniment louder."

At the end of an hour Justin was wet with perspiration, Hester was aglow with triumph and they looked at each other in amazement.

"Do you know you just got a good tone?" she asked. "Oh, I'm thrilled!"

"If I weren't a man I think I would cry," he said. "How can I ever, ever thank you!"

"By doing it regularly until you've really won the mastery. You know now it's possible. That's what will make all the difference in your efforts."

"But you? You can't — "

"Just can't I? If you knew how empty in many ways my life has been, evenings most of all. Now at a time when you're not writing, we're going to practice. And this will be my salvation, really! I mean it."

"Perhaps I'll give the book a rest for a little. Maybe I've been trying too hard. The practice may be my salvation too. But in any case, I haven't words or thoughts fine enough to thank you. And you must never have me on your mind, as it were. Then I would have to stop. I must leave now before you are worn out completely."

"Shall we say day after tomorrow? About three? You musn't lose what you've learned, you know. Would it suit?"

"Any time would suit and I'll be practically living to make sure I didn't dream that last note, and for other reasons too," he added.

"Fine! And that will get me out of a long, hot bridge game. So see what you're doing for me."

As he left he held her hand gently. "Good night, little ship. I can't say how grateful I am for everything. Perhaps memory, most of all!"

Westbrook was definitely not a secretive town. While it would not be fair to call it gossipy, there was, within its citizenry, a very strong interest in the activities of its neighbors. This was, in the main, a friendly interest, tempered here and there with a shrewd criticism. So when the news spread rapidly that John Justin was making frequent calls upon Hester Carr, there was conversation aplenty. The women, as a whole, were pleased. They all liked Hester, had always, in fact, liked her better than Walter. They knew how lonely she had been. As born matchmakers, they considered the present situation a gift from heaven. The men also liked Hester, but counseled caution (by way of their wives), saying that while they also liked Justin the whole thing seemed a little precipitous, that is, if it was true he went to see her nearly every day. *"After all — "* they said, leaving the sentence unfinished.

As to Hester herself, knowing her friends, knowing the town, she set out early to clear up the clouds of surmise which she knew would be rising. Beginning with Ginny and a few close friends, she explained earnestly just what was happening. Justin was working on his violin while she accompanied and encouraged him. He had given it up because of the stiff fingers and now he was really making progress. She was so happy she could help him. That was all there was to it and she would certainly thank them not to be getting wild ideas in their heads, etc., etc. It was all in vain. They stared at her with delighted countenances, with Ginny exploding at intervals in such remarks as "But doesn't it almost seem foreordained? Oh, you know, just as though it was to be!"

And the other girls, smiling their happy, matchmaking smiles and trying their best to be casual, said in various ways, of course, it was a wonderful opportunity for Mr. Justin to work on his violin and such nice company for Hester and had he really *never* been married? Strange, when he was so terribly attractive, and so on and on.

Hester gave up her explanations. The truth was that she was enjoying herself more than she had ever done in her life. There was the slow but steady triumph with the tones of the violin, in which she rejoiced as much as did John. They had advanced to first names quickly. There were the long autumnal walks with Flushie when he trotted ahead of them, delighted. When he lagged once, Hester said, "I pick him up when he gets tired. Couldn't you carry him, John?"

"Why should I? He has more legs than I have." But he turned at once to go back while Hester laughed at his whimsy. Indeed, there was always much laughter between them, at which Hester marveled. Small things as well as larger provided occasion for merriment. Justin himself spoke of it once.

"I think I was a sort of desiccated old fossil when I arrived here. I enjoyed the students, many of them, and we had a good deal of humor back and forth between us at times, but having *fun* such as I have with you — and with Flushie and Hattie too," he added, "is quite a different matter. I feel as though I were limbering up all over, not just my stiff fingers."

"I love the fun too. I have had spots of it with the girls, of course, but not quite like this. I thank you."

"Not like this?" he asked in surprise.

"Not exactly," she said quietly.

When they reached the house again after their walks, Hattie was usually on the lookout for them and lost no time in speaking her mind.

"Now just come right in, both of you. There's no sense, Mr. Justin, in you goin' home to a scrappy meal by yourself when I've got a good dinner all ready."

"But I'm ashamed, Hattie. It seems I'm always having

dinner here and I haven't enough will power to refuse."

"Get along with you! Wash up, both of you, while I'm feeding the pup an' then you can sit down to an early dinner an' get at your fiddle in good time. I must say, it's soundin' a good deal better than it did."

"There's glory for you," Hester said, "and you'd better do just as Hattie says or she'll likely wash your face herself." And there was more laughter.

One morning the air was unusually warm and summery, the breeze lighthearted and playful. Hester woke with the spirit of the breeze and had an immediate strange thought. She wanted to go on a picnic. Not for years had she sat on a blanket by a running stream and eaten from a wicker basket. Walter had loathed picnics and cared little for even the most sophisticated cookouts. She knew the very place to go, too, for she had often watched it longingly. She sprang from bed, dislodging Flushie under the coverlet, and reached the phone. She never called Justin except for important reasons. Now, as his voice answered a trifle uneasily, she hastened to speak brightly.

"John, would you care to go for a picnic today? Just you and Flushie and I? We couldn't leave him out. Would you even consider it?"

"I will give it my earnest attention, but I am a man for facts. What do we do? Where do we go? I can't remember when I ever was at such a thing. Tell me why you woke up as early as this, imbued with the idea of going on a picnic."

Hester laughed. "Because I'm a little bit crazy. I've wanted to picnic along the banks of a shady stream I know for years. But I didn't dare suggest it to the girls for at once it would grow into a crowd and then probably a cookout! I want a quiet spot with gentle ripples from the water and a light breeze like today to move the branches. This morning is just right. What do you think?"

"You really want to know?"

Hester held her breath. "Yes."

"Then I'd love it. I'll get into my clothes and be around for you. How soon? I'm sort of in a hurry to show off my new car again!"

"Make it nine and then we'll have breakfast together and can supervise the basket packing. If we don't watch Hattie, she'll have a roast of beef in it. Oh John, you are so good to agree to go!"

There was a pause and then Justin's voice came quietly. "*I* am good!" he said. "You open golden doors to me and tell me I'm good because I walk through them. I repeat, I'm going to love this picnic."

After a hearty breakfast and careful packing of the basket, Flushie, curling into double knots for joy before his own particular golden doors, was installed on his blanket on the back seat beside an extra rug and the lunch itself.

"Have we forgotten anything?" Hester asked before she got in the car.

"Just our dignity and it's well lost." Justin chuckled.

They drove past the golf course, away beyond the hills that screened Sackville from its elegant neighbor, up a long winding road, down slowly into a small valley with its beauties at first hidden by low trees and sumac bushes.

"Could you park here?" Hester said where the road widened slightly, "for I want you to come on the little spot of beauty suddenly. I've claimed it for my own for a long time, but I'm going to share it with you today."

They walked a little distance from the car and there, at a small break in the bushes, Hester pulled them aside as Justin helped her, then stood quiet except for a soft exclamation of pleasure. Below a grassy bank flowed a small stream. It was clear with glints of light touching it as it ran, unhurried, on its way. Rounded stones of an incredibly soft sandy brown color caught the ripples as they passed and occasionally made small rainbows as the light and water met. There was a faint, soothing sound from the stream as though it had made its onlookers its friends; and like a frame on either side were the sumac bushes and the small patient little trees waiting to grow up.

Hester looked at Justin who still didn't speak, while Flushie waited, wagged his tail and watched them both. At last she said, "Well?"

He drew a long sigh and smiled. "This is idyllic. I'm afraid I'll suddenly wake up and it will all have disappeared. Thank you for bringing me," he added and his voice told the rest.

Hester became businesslike. She spread the rug, fastened Flushie's chain at a good length to a young tree, set the basket at a safe distance and then sat down to enjoy the little valley which she loved. Justin sat beside her and, still without speaking, watched all the details about him with eyes that feasted upon them.

"I don't know when I've felt such utter peace," he said at last. "This little stream is so different from the famous 'Brook,' isn't it?"

"Oh dear, yes! I would never have enjoyed staying long

beside it as it chattered, chattered. But here there is only a soft, gentle, enticing sound — " She stopped and looked roguishly at her companion. "I'm going to do something I've longed to do for years, if you won't tell on me!"

"It sounds a bit ominous, but I guess I can trust you. And, of course I'll keep your secret to the grave. Tell me in a hurry, though. I can't bear the suspense."

"Well," Hester said, taking off her sandals, "I'm going across the stream on the stones!"

"But you mustn't. Some of them may be slippery. I don't approve of that at all."

"I shouldn't have told you until I was halfway over. It's perfectly safe and I've longed for ages to do it."

"Why didn't you?"

"Oh, different reasons. Now, you see, I've become obstinate." She laughed a little.

"Of course," he said, rising, "I can stand on the edge and be ready to fish you out if you fall in. But do be careful."

The stones were of assorted sizes, but while not in line, of course, they were not too far apart, some showing large above the water, some underneath with the twinkling light of the ripples playing over them. Hester gave instructions to Flushie to stay still and be quiet, then started down the long grassy bank, with Justin following.

"You *could* slip and sprain an ankle," he warned.

"Now don't make dire predictions and spoil my fun. I'm about to fulfill a long suppressed desire. You don't have to watch me if you don't want to," she added.

"Oh, as if I could miss *that!*" he said. "Well, go ahead if you must and good luck. I'll be here if you need me."

Hester tested the water with one foot and moved from a

small stone at the edge to the big rounded one that showed from all sides. It felt warm and smooth. She stayed a few moments, scanning the course ahead. Then, slowly, carefully, with one or two near misses, she moved with short steps and longer ones over the stones and across the stream. When she reached the other side, Justin shouted "Hurrah!" Flushie apparently felt he was free then to bark and Hester herself stood with her arms outstretched and called out her triumph.

"It was *wonderful!* All I dreamed it would be. And now I'm going to do something still more daring. I'm going to *wade over!*"

"Oh, I don't think that's a good idea. You'd better come back the way you went. There are sure to be mossy spots underneath and the water certainly has a little depth to it."

"It could come about to my knees. I'm glad I wore shorts. Now you and Flushie keep quiet and watch me. This is another old desire, so I'm terribly obdurate. Here I come!"

She stepped slowly into the water as though actually savoring it. Slowly, carefully, she made her way, pausing every little while to look, entranced, at the glinting sunlight through the leaves and to listen to the soft, throaty ripple of the stream, drawing as she did so, long breaths of delight.

She finally reached the other side and grasped Justin's outstretched hands. She stood on the grassy bank, her face filled with a sort of rapture.

"The beauty of it!" she said. "It was all lovelier even than I dreamed it would be, there in the water. It seemed to me as though the whole world was new and I myself was just now freshly created."

Justin bowed. "Madam, I am Adam," he said politely.

For a second she did not catch the joke. When she did, she threw back her head and laughed until the small dell rang with it.

"The sweetest sound since Eden, I'm sure," Justin murmured.

"That's so *funny,*" Hester gasped. "So incredibly clever of you to think of it! However did you? Oh, I must sit down or I'll laugh myself back into the water."

Once again seated upon the blanket, they gave way to mirth. "But tell me," he asked once more, "since you wanted for so long to do this, why didn't you?"

Hester looked embarrassed. "Walter, my husband, would not have approved. But not for your reasons," she said quietly and then began to talk quickly about the delicious feel of the water and the fact that she had begun to be hungry in spite of Hattie's breakfast.

They ate the picnic slowly, looking much at the gentle stream and often at each other. There was, indeed, more meaning in their glances than there had ever been before. When Hester found herself blushing, she turned quickly on pretext of feeding Flushie part of her sandwich.

"He's so dear to me," she observed. "I tremble to think what I would do if something happened to him. Dogs' lives are too short. Their only fault, really. I'm always a little nervous about Bill, from Sackville. Every time he comes to do a bit of work about the place, he eyes Flushie enviously and wants to buy him. Imagine!"

Justin at once looked grave. "I've been thinking about Sackville lately," he said. "Their school begins next week. They have a rummy little old two-story brick building, the inside divided into what are known as 'the little room' and 'the big room,' not from the size of its space, but the age of the children."

Hester giggled. "That's amusing, really."

"Amusing, yes, to anyone but the kids. It's rather tragic for them. I met the new principal yesterday, he who will teach 'the big room,' and if I ever saw a scared rabbit he was it. He's afraid of those big boys. They are a tough lot, he says, and carried the last principal out bodily. The thing I've been wondering is whether I could possibly lend a hand."

"You? Why John, what could you do?"

"Oh, I don't know. Maybe nothing, but I've been thinking — this may sound ridiculous to you."

"No," Hester said quickly, "please tell me everything. It will certainly not seem ridiculous if you have thought of it."

"Well, it's like this. It's a lousy little town, always has been" — he caught himself quickly — "as I've heard. They have no interest in education or money to pay for good teachers. The County Superintendent, or whoever should bolster it up, evidently thinks it's hopeless and looks the other way. Now my idea is that amongst those older boys there just could be a few who would be interested in music, let's say. Maybe I could work up a little fife and drum corps if I got the instruments. If I once got their good will I might even be able to make an English class have some meaning to them. I needn't add that though this all seems a bit crazy, I'm itching to try. What — what do you think, honestly?"

Hester's face was tender. "The idea is wonderful and

somehow I believe it will work. What about the girls?"

"Oh, a chorus, maybe. I really know a little about music, though from my violin renderings just now you might not think so."

"Oh, you couldn't fool me on that. I knew the first night at Ginny's when you read the notes we all knew by heart. Did you tell your scared rabbit of your plan?"

"I couldn't resist, for he looked so pathetic. When he heard me he clutched my arm like a man saved from drowning. He says the opening session, he hears, is likely to be pretty rough and if I'd only be there and let him introduce me and have me make — God save the mark — a little speech, he thinks he would have a chance to get on with things. Of course," he added grinning, "I may be the one that gets carried out."

It was Hester's face now that was grave. She clasped her hands about her knees and looked off into the little valley.

"It has only just come to me now how selfish we have all been about Sackville. We've been glad to have the women wash or clean for us and the men do odd jobs about our yards — one man is the only person around who can really prune a grapevine properly. Of course, we pay them, but it ends there. We're always relieved to see them go back to Sackville and stay there. And yet," she added musingly, "we women at our church sew for the Red Cross and raise money for foreign missions. It took you, a stranger, to make me see what lies under my very eyes. John, if your plan works and I think it will, count on me for anything. Is there a piano in the school?"

"I asked Brown, the principal, about that. He says

there's a battered old thing one of the men got hold of once. I'm going to check it. If it was properly tuned, it might work. You don't mean you'd really — "

"Of course I do. But Ginny would be the best at the piano, for she can do the jazzy stuff to perfection. Then I could fill in with the steady 'Give me the key of C, please.' You'll need a lot of that. Am I free to broach the matter to Ginny? She has a very kind heart."

"Yes," he said slowly. "If we can just mention it casually to a few people without making a big thing of it, it might really be helpful. The only cause for secrecy would be if the plan didn't work. How would it be if we would hold everything until after that first day of school? You see, I can sound the boys out a little then."

So it was agreed. They packed the picnic things slowly and stood for a time silently on the bank, each feeling that in some strange way there had come a turning point in their relationship. Justin spoke first. "This has been one of the happiest days of my life," he said, "and there is something I would like to tell you now before we leave this lovely spot. For certain reasons, I can't. Would you be willing to allow our friendship to continue just as it is for a little longer?"

Hester raised her eyes to his. "Of course," she said. "It's a beautiful friendship, I think."

"Thank you," he answered. His lips smiled but his eyes were misty.

On the Monday morning of Sackville's first day of school, John Justin was more nervous than he had ever been over any Harvard exam. His hands were unsteady as he tied his tie. He had forgone Hattie's breakfast for he wanted to be alone and concentrate upon what he was about to do. Also, he intended to reach "the big room" as soon as Brown, the principal, did. This hour was to be seven-thirty. "They start to come at eight," Brown reported, "and it may be bedlam."

As Justin swallowed his coffee and a roll, he tried to picture the scene and the sounds — and shuddered. He decided to park his car on Hester's street and walk over. When he reached the unkempt yard surrounding the schoolhouse, a group of big boys were already there. They stopped shouting and eyed him suspiciously. Justin raised his hand.

"Hi!" he said, and waited.

The boys looked at each other as though waiting for a leader to indicate the course of action. A tall, bony youth with full cheeks belying the rest of his body structure finally answered, "Hi" and the others followed.

"What are you doin' here?" the leader asked.

"I hardly know," Justin said smiling, hoping his nervousness didn't show through. "Your new principal, Mr. Brown — "

> Brown, Brown,
> We'll bring him down
> An' run him out of town;
> Brown, Brown, Brown!

the tall one chanted at once to the glee of the others.

"Why, you're quite a poet!" Justin said. "I don't believe you could make a rhyme on my name though. It's John Justin."

With only a second's hesitation, the boy said:

John, John the Justin's son
Stole a pig and away he run;
Old Justin beat his little son
John, John, the Justin's son!

"There's one line in it I didn't make up myself," he added apologetically. "The rest ain't so bad."

Justin chuckled. "I think it was great. Someday I predict you'll be making real poetry. Now I've got to go in. Do you cats like school?"

There was a dead hush while the boys looked at each other. Justin was embarrassed.

"I'm sorry," he said. "The boys I teach often call each other cats, but I won't say it if you don't like it."

A small boy at the end of the group all but shouted his response. "But we *do* like it. That's what we call ourselves too, only the old folks never — "

"Yeah," broke in the bony leader, "we're a bunch of cool cats all right and we *don't like school.* It stinks!"

"Yes," Justin agreed. "It does sometimes. But something nice could happen. Give us a chance."

"Are you goin' to teach or something?"

"I'm taking a year off from teaching while I try to write a book. It's not going too well, so I have some extra time. I thought of something the other day that might be fun for you boys. So," he added, "don't throw us out till we have a try at it, will you? O.K.? For a while?"

The leader scanned his followers and then said grudgingly, "O.K., for a while."

Justin went on into the schoolhouse and climbed the narrow wooden stairs worn into hollows by several generations of stomping feet. At one spot he stood still while his head dropped to his breast. Then he drew a long breath and went on to meet Brown who, at his desk, was buried in dog-eared textbooks. There were new tablets and pencils, however. All at once, more shouts rose from the playground and swarms of older children entered the room with suspicious eyes fixed on the men at the front.

"I think you'd better tell them your plan right away," Brown said. "I'm getting more nervous by the minute."

"Keep your chin up, old man," Justin encouraged him. "They may be better than they look."

On the stroke of nine the confusion became worse confounded as the big boys pounded up the stairs and slouched as noisily as possible into the back seats from which there rose at once an epidemic of coughing so loud that any voice would be drowned by it. Also, homemade slingshots of rubber bands were produced and with spitballs for ammunition, aim was taken with deadly accuracy. When one such hit Brown squarely on the nose, Justin stood up.

"While you are getting settled, suppose we have a song or two. The piano's been tuned. I can't play much, for I have a couple of stiff fingers. Auto accident."

"Drivin' with one hand, I suppose?" came from one of the big boys.

Justin merely smiled as the laughter rose to a roar and subsided. Then he said quite seriously, "No, as a matter of fact, I wasn't. I had both hands on the wheel, but at an intersection where I had the right of way a fellow who was either drunk or crazy hit me broadside. I'm lucky to be alive. Well, what do you want to sing?"

"My country tizzle thee," one girl at the front volunteered.

"Good!" Justin struck a chord and raised the tune himself. To his surprise, Brown had a strong, clear tenor. He stood now, Justin could see with a glance, squarely upright and determined of posture, his nose still red from the missile, his whole face scarlet also and an angry flash from his eyes.

"Gad!" Justin thought to himself, with an inward chuckle, "that was just what was needed to set him on fire. If anybody gets thrown out now, I don't believe after all it will be Brown."

By the third verse, even the big boys were bellowing and Justin's keen ear caught a good note here and there. It was evident they had not had a chance to sing before.

"Let's have another! Yeah, give us another."

They moved from old folk songs evidently heard from their cradles in the shabby houses of Sackville to the newer ones which had come over the scattered radios there.

They sang "Easy on My Mind" and "Raindrops Are Falling on My Head," but when they asked for the newest of all, Justin had to give up. He rose and explained that he didn't know the latest songs and anyway they had probably taken up enough time for the first morning, and sat down. Brown took over with an astonishing air of confidence, evidently not lost on the pupils before him.

"Before we begin any sort of work," he said, "I want to introduce a guest, a very distinguished guest who is with us this morning."

He proceeded then to the guest's embarrassment, to give

a detailed report of Justin's academic accomplishments, dwelling heavily on the Rhodes scholarship, even pausing to answer a question or two. At the end he said, "Mr. Justin is having a year off from his college work and is staying in Westbrook while he writes a book. He is very interested in young people and in schools in general and has some ideas that I think may interest you. We will give him our best attention." With a bow, "Professor Justin."

Justin rose and scanned the room from his nearer vantage point. He plunged in at once on his plan, explaining that while everyone at their various ages had to go to school, he knew by experience it could get a bit monotonous. There were groans from the back seats.

"So," Justin went on, "I've thought of something that might be fun to do on the side and a little educational too."

He explained the idea of the Drum and Fife corps and the boys' mouths fell open with interest.

"Do you like the idea?"

They all looked at Bony as their leader to make the reply. He swallowed a couple of times as though speech for once was difficult.

"Don't sound too bad," he managed at last.

"Can anyone in Sackville beat a drum?"

There were quick answers. "Sure, Snecky Webb used to beat one all the time till one of the kids put his foot through it. Snecky give him hell but it didn't fix the drum. Snecky's been sort of sickly ever since."

"But if he had a new one he could maybe show some of you boys how to do it?"

"Oh sure," said Bony, regaining his aplomb. "He could

even do those here ruffles or whatever you call them. Dunno where he learnt how."

"Good!" said Justin. "We'll discuss the fife again. I would like you older boys to select three among you as a sort of committee to talk with me tomorrow afternoon and get things lined up. Could we meet here, Mr. Brown, about four-thirty? . . . Thank you, that's settled, then. Now, as to the girls — "

He looked over the wistful faces before him, judging rightly that the many pasty cheeks may have been caused by scanty breakfasts.

"I think there's material here for a fine chorus. I listened carefully while we were singing and I heard some good voices. You could all be in a chorus, you know, and since I know some music I could train you. I think you'd enjoy it."

There was a quick, general intaking of breaths, as though the pleasure glimpsed was too wonderful for speech.

"Fine, then," Justin said, smiling upon them. "Now, I must go and let you get on with your work. Thank you, Mr. Brown. You have a nice group of young people here and they are lucky to have a teacher like you."

He started to the back of the room with a gesture of farewell. At the door, however, he paused and, as he stood for a moment looking over the faces turned toward him, he was no longer the easygoing pal, as it were, of the older boys; he was a strong man of authority, accustomed to having his commands obeyed.

"There's one thing I should state very clearly," he said. "If our plans work out, I think you will all have some fun and some pleasure. But if any boys or girls make trouble in this room or do not study when they have the chance, they're *out.* We don't want that kind. Let's pull together and make a go of it."

He left a quiet room behind him and went slowly down the stairs, holding to the scuffed hand rail. He was shaky. He knew now that it had not only been Brown who was scared. He had been more tense himself than he had realized. If Hattie has any available food, I won't refuse this time, he thought. Besides, I want to tell all the news to Hester.

He climbed the little hill which served as a barrier between Sackville and Westbrook, stopping once to scan the street behind him. A number of men, with apparently no work, sat on their rickety front steps, smoking pipes and looking vacantly ahead of them while their wives hung out washings or worked the gardens.

"The lazy louts!" Justin muttered to himself. "They could clean up that whole place if they had a mind to do it."

He finally struck the Avenue and turned down Hester's own street. His heart beat faster and he monitored it sternly. Not yet, not yet, must the word *love* be spoken or even thought of because of possible disaster falling upon it. He must hold himself in readiness to bear that if it came. Meanwhile, bless the poets! If he quoted them with a light enough touch, they could speak for him with a sort of ambivalence.

He reached the house, now dearly familiar, and found a warm welcome waiting. Flushie rushed upon him and Hattie spoke with authority.

"I'll wager you hadn't much breakfast," she said accusingly.

"Some coffee and a dried-up roll, but surely I'm not hinting."

"Well, get yourself upstairs and wash up. It's only ten now an' Miss Hester here hasn't had anything but coffee. You said you'd not be too long over there so I've a good breakfast all ready. Scrub your hands well, mind, for that Sackville's a nest of germs. When Bill eats anything here when he's workin' I scald the dishes. I'll be settin' things out."

Hester and Justin laughed together as he ran up the stairs. "I can't wait for the news," she called after him. "Generally good or bad — just a word."

"I think good."

When they were seated at the table, at Hester's insistence, he satisfied his first hunger, confessed to having been more shaky than Brown himself and then, settled to Hattie's second helpings, told all the morning's conversation as he remembered it. Hester listened, asked questions now and then, her eyes shining into his.

"I'll try to find this Snecky, the drummer, this afternoon. If he's willing to tackle that end of it, provided I can find him a new drum, he'll be a gift from heaven."

"He's a dirty, filthy old man," Hattie interjected from the doorway. "If you go down to where he lives, keep your distance, for pity's sake. He lives with his daughter and her two kids an' she don't pay no attention to him. He's been poorly, they say, ever since the kids broke his drum."

"What about the husband?"

Hattie had the grace to look embarrassed. She looked at Hester and then at Justin.

"Husband," she snorted self-righteously. "She hasn't got one. She began way back when she was sixteen, takin' the easy way I guess it's called — "

"Hattie!" Hester objected.

"Well, he might as well know the kind of place he's gettin' into. The women that come up here to work say they wouldn't be surprised to find this Liz, that's her name, murdered in her bed someday. They get so scunnered seein' some of the money they need to keep body an' soul together goin' to Liz. Ugh! Men!" Hattie exclaimed with violent distaste, but added, "Of course, I don't mean *you,* Mr. Justin."

"Thank you," he said. "We can just stick to the generic term then."

"Whatever that is, an' I've a fresh pan of muffins just ready to take out. Since it's this time of day, you an' Miss Hester might as well make this brunch."

When she had gone back to the kitchen, Hester looked at Justin, her color high. "I'm truly ashamed for I never know what she's going to say next. Yet, how could I live without her?"

"Don't try," he said, laughing. "It was really very funny for I think she was warning me for fear I'd get seduced. Have you ever seen the siren yourself?"

"Once or twice when she's come up here with one of the other women. She will condescend to help serve a dinner occasionally, but won't do any harder work. The striking thing is that she's very, very pretty, which, I imagine, doesn't make her any more popular with the other women whose looks show they've led hard lives."

"Quite a story there," Justin said thoughtfully. "Well, I can't thank you enough for the brunch. I was definitely in need of nourishment. Now I must be on my way either to talk with Snecky or go on hunt of a drum. I don't know which should come first. What do you think?"

Hester considered. "If the old man has been pining away for his drum, I believe I'd start with that. Take it along as an introduction. I've heard he's pretty irascible and otherwise he might not even give you a hearing."

"I'm sure you're right. I'll try the village here and if that's no go, I'll start into the city tomorrow. But where would one go to buy a drum? I'll need more than one at that."

"Have you ever been to Bostwick's Hardware?"

"Never heard of it."

"You have an interesting surprise coming then, if you go. The hardware name has stuck for several generations but you can find anything there. I'll venture, in some far recess, they might even have a drum. It's worth a try before you make a trip to the city. It's an incredible place, really. Not exactly in Westbrook village, but a little way beyond on the main road."

"I suppose you wouldn't care to act as a guide?"

"I've been shamelessly hoping to be asked. Wait until I tell Hattie and say good-bye to Flushie."

Once on their way, Justin spoke more freely of his plan. "Those kids are starved for beauty, for some sort of expression other than kicking tin cans around the lot. I'm going to give this the best I've got. If it fails, well — "

"It isn't going to fail," Hester said confidently, "and I've been doing some thinking on my own. If you get the boys to the point of playing a little tune and marching to it, I'll see they have uniforms. That would make the whole thing dramatic for them. Ginny and some of the other women would go in with me. Wouldn't that be fun?"

"It would be marvelous and so are you."

"Here we are," Hester said, indicating a large, rambling, unpainted building. Once inside there was silence amongst the vast miscellany of stock, although a feeble bell had announced their presence. At last an old man with a fringe of white hair at his forehead and a large quid of tobacco in his cheek emerged warily from the back room and surveyed them, then called behind him.

"Strangers, Gus. Guess I'll have to stay out, gol' darn it! We was just in the midst of a game of checkers," he explained to his customers. "Well, can't be helped. What can I do for you?"

Justin had difficulty controlling his risibility, but managed to say, "A drum."

The old man scratched his head thoughtfully, apparently finding nothing unusual in the request. "Well, now 'pears to me 'bout three year ago some of the men in the village here got an idee for a big parade on the Fourth of July an' they ordered several drums. Then the whole thing fell through an' we just kep' them. If you keep things long enough, some fool or other will come along an' buy 'em. These here drums are up in the attic there an' you climb up the ladder to get to it. You look soople, young man. I got rheumatiz. Do you want to go up an' have a look?"

"I certainly do," Justin said quickly.

"That ladder's about as good as stairs, I will say. It's easy climbin' an' the drums are at the front there."

"Take care, John," Hester warned. But the ascent was easily made and Justin came down with the ribbon of one drum over his arm.

"This is perfect," he said excitedly. "I'll want those other two. Have you someone who will get them down this afternoon?"

"Yep. Got a delivery boy comin'. Jupiter jeebes, I forgot what we paid for the things. Charge you a dollar an' a half for each. O.K.?"

"It doesn't seem enough. And I'll probably want more. Can you order what I need?"

"Sure, sure! Don't know what they'll cost, but you can have these for what I said. Glad to get rid of them. What you want 'em for?" he asked curiously.

"Oh, for some boys," Justin responded.

"Good. Boys always hanker after drums. Well, thank you kindly," as Justin passed over the money and gave his address.

"Tell the boy to leave them on the porch," he said, "and now get back to your checkers."

"By jumpin' jiminy, I'd forgot them an' me almost in the King Row. I'll bet I beat him yet."

When Justin and Hester were again in the car with their treasure, their conversation ran together in ecstatic little sentences. This first incredible find did seem like a good omen, indeed, and they talked the plan all over from every angle.

"I think I'll let you out at your house," Justin said, "and

go straight on to find this Snecky. Could I drive into Sackville? Would an automobile cause too much excitement?"

"Oh, there are plenty of old rackety ones there. A car like this of yours might cause some interest, but no trouble, I'm sure. Just be sure to take the drum with you when you get out."

Justin drove warily down the Sackville street when he finally reached it, and stopped before the last house in the shabby row as he had been directed. As he did he straightened in surprise, listening. A woman's voice, a rich contralto, came from somewhere within. Every note was clear, effortless and true.

> No shadows yonder,
> All is light and song;
> Each day I wonder,
> And say, how long —

The last lines were not distinguishable as the singer evidently moved toward the back of the house as she sang. Justin drew a deep breath. What a voice! And what words to be emanating from the Sackville street. He remembered them vaguely from years past. As he got out of the car with the drum, there was one final burst of song.

No shadows yonder!

Then all was quiet. Justin moved up the uneven steps to the door and saw the object of his search sitting inside. He was dirty (at least his face, as Hattie had predicted), unshaven, and slumped in a posture of despair. Justin spoke, introduced himself and stepped in. The old man opened his bleary eyes and caught sight of the drum.

"What you got there?" he asked with surprising strength.

"It's for you if you'll do me a big favor," Justin replied as he handed it over.

The change in the old man was electrical. He sat up straight, took the drum on his knee, carefully released the sticks from the side where they had been anchored and began a soft tattoo which, Justin recognized at once, took skill.

Snecky drew long breaths as though coming from unconsciousness back to life. "How come you brought this to me? Stranger here, ain't you?"

Justin drew up one of the straight chairs, sat down and told his plan in detail. Snecky listened with interest, the while keeping up a very soft accompaniment on the drum.

"Sure I can teach a few of the kids if they've got any idee of keepin' time. You gotta' have that. 'Loyshus, my grandson, has some music in him. He could learn if he wasn't so all-fired stubborn."

"Someone here has a lovely voice. I heard it as I stopped the car."

Snecky looked startled. "Oh, *her.* That's Liz. She's my daughter. She's always singin'. 'Loyshus can sing pretty good too, when the maggot bites him. Well, thank ya' kindly for the drum. It's put new life in me an' I'll help some of the kids if they have the guts to stick at it. Takes practice, you know. I learnt it from my Gran'pap. He was in the Civil War. Drummer."

When Justin was again in his car, he listened intently, but the voice he had heard before was silent. What sort of story was back of all this? For surely, the singer must be the Scarlet Woman whom Hattie had described with such venom, or was it relish? He knew enough to realize that the voice, though untrained, was magnificent in quality. What might the owner of it not have done with it if she were not keeping house for an old man and her "children of shame," as Hattie delicately dubbed them in her final description.

He declined more food when he reached the Carr home, after giving the details of Snecky's reception of the drum. "I've got to get back now and plan just what I'm going to say at this so-called committee meeting tomorrow afternoon. Things have gone so well this far, I'm a little bit scared. I'll have to be prepared for some hurdles. So, I'll tell you all the news after I have my talk with the boys."

"Tomorrow night's your fiddle practice," Hattie reminded, from the back hall, "an' I'm plannin' on chicken an' spoon bread for dinner."

"There," he said, "I'm weak as water when Hattie starts on her menus. All right. I'll accept with pleasure for tomorrow and then I've got to discipline myself and not stay so often for meals. It's really indecent. I'm becoming a boarder."

When Hattie was back in the kitchen, Justin looked down at Hester as she walked out with him to the porch.

"Of course, my temptation does not lie chiefly in the meals, wonderful as they are. You must realize that, I think. Last night I spent the evening with the poets and came up with some gems I hadn't remembered. Here is one that is apropos to the present conversation.

> I saw you every day and all the day:
> And every day was still but as the first;
> So eager was I still to see you more.

"Pretty sentimental for old John Dryden and me, isn't it? Well, I'll see you then." He stooped to caress Flushie, gave a smiling wave and went to his car.

All the way back to his house he kept thinking of the sun on Hester's hair and of whether the lines he had lightly quoted would still seem to her too expressive of his real feelings. Then there came over him again his amazement as he had heard The Voice and the strange words it sang with such apparent feeling. He must sometime have heard the song, but it had been lost in multiple layers of memory.

No shadows yonder,
All is light and song

Well, there were plenty of shadows in Sackville. He only hoped that his unlikely scheme might lift a few of them from some of the young hearts.

CHAPTER FOUR

JUSTIN had been right in his presentiments. The impulsive plan to bring a mingling of pleasure and culture to the barren young lives of Sackville had, it now seemed, started off too smoothly, too well. After the first "committee" meetings, the arrival of the drums with their attendant excitement, the demonstration by Justin of what could be done on a recorder and also on a little half-instrument, half-toy affair which he had found in the city — one with limited range but shrill, pipelike notes which the boys praised inordinately — after all this there had at first been an enthusiasm bordering upon zeal itself. Then, slowly, surely, the reaction set in.

Snecky made it increasingly and profanely clear to his pupils that it was going to take steady practice to learn to beat a drum properly. Justin also explained to the players of the recorders and the "fifettes" that they would have to work on them every day in order to achieve even a simple tune. Came then the lull, led by Bony.

"Aw, I dunno how we ever got into this here mess. I don't want to be beatin' the damned drum. I'd druther be out playin' shinny."

"Me too." There was a chorus.

"I tried for an hour to get a tune out of that there recorder thing and I couldn't do it. What does he think we are? Musicians or something? I'm quittin'."

There were general sounds of agreement which unfortunately Justin heard as he came around the schoolhouse. His heart sank. He could have explained to no one the tremendous elation which had filled him before: neither could he now admit to the sick disappointment within him at the collapse of his dream. With inherent wisdom he decided not to urge the boys to change their minds. This was not the time, if ever. These young males were tough, determined, completely arrogant in their own self-willed way. They were not like their counterparts in Westbrook who might, at a crisis, be cajoled or reasoned with. So now, Justin turned back.

Amidst the general debacle of the plans, there was one small, saved remnant. This was the girls' chorus. As though having longed for and been denied any decent release for their emotions, they now poured them into song, usually too loud and often off key, but with a sort of craving zest. They were all there for each rehearsal, eager in their untutored way to follow Justin's baton and accept his patient criticism and suggestion. The boys, often lurking outside but within earshot, teased them unmercifully, sending up ribald remarks and verses during the break of the song. The Poet, as Justin dubbed him, had achieved one quatrain which evidently took the boys' fancy, for over and over it was hurled through the high windows:

> Girls! Girls! Girls!
> With platted hair an' mebbe curls
> Singin' in a *chorus!*
> Lord have mercy o'er us.

When the boys were reprimanded, they looked at each other in blank amazement and with faces devoid of guile.

"It's been some of them snotty brats from the Little Room that's done it. Wasn't us, was it?" said Bony.

"We never done nothin'," the rest echoed.

So the remarks and verses continued, but the perpetrators were never caught. When either Brown or Justin went out to admonish them, they had melted away like dew in the sun.

"How do they disappear so quickly?" Justin asked once.

"Oh, it's a sort of protective technique they've learned," answered Brown, who, in a short time, had learned a good deal about Sackville techniques himself.

The girls' attitude toward the vocal salutes was a calm one. Some of their own remarks measured up quite well to those of the boys, but were given in guarded tones with an eye on Justin.

"It aren't the little boys that's doin' it," one especially mild girl explained. "It's them damned bastards from our own room here, Mr. Justin," she said, with her sweetest smile.

It had, indeed, been the girls who had nonplused Justin

to the greatest degree. He knew boys in general, but girls were a closed book to him. These of Sackville, skinny or buxom, now in their mid-teens, looked upon him, he was relieved to see, with respect, but also with open admiration and even longing, which made his face burn. For some reason, Brown seemed to escape the latter. So Justin had gone patiently on with the training until finally the beginnings of harmony emerged. At this point, he had meant to ask Hester and Ginny also to come to the rehearsals to provide accompaniments. When the boys had begun in the smallest degree to show improvement, he would beg the pianists to give them some support also. Now, nothing was left of the Great Plan but the chorus, which was indeed a sort of afterthought. It was the *boys* Justin had so longed to reach. His heart was sore now with hope defeated. For he could not convince himself that the future would bring any change of attitude.

He delayed telling the devastating news to Hester. But after she had studied his drawn face and watched his forced smile and carefully worded answers to her questions, she looked gravely at him one evening. "I thought we were friends," she said.

"I should hope so," he answered quickly.

"True friends may confide in each other. I know you're troubled. Is it about Sackville?"

"I'm ashamed not to have told you at once. The truth is, I've been so low-spirited I couldn't talk about my disappointment just yet, even to you. I hope you will forgive me."

"I'll try," Hester said, "if you tell me all, now."

"Here it is, then, in a nutshell. My Great Scheme, my Shining Hope for Sackville's youth, has fallen through. Done. Finished. When the boys found it was going to take work to achieve results, they wanted no more practice. They elected to play shinny. The recorders, all but one which we couldn't trace, and the fifettes, as we call the other things, are at present in my living room. The drums are in a locked closet at school. The boys are kicking tin cans as usual."

"And the chorus? Is it all disbanded too?" she asked eagerly.

"Heavens, no! You couldn't stop those girls if you tried. When they heard that the boys were giving up, they begged, they pleaded with me to go on. I suppose I'll have to, though I haven't much stomach for it."

Hester pushed her coffee cup aside and leaned over the table, looking steadily at the man beside her.

"You set out to help the Sackville boys, that is true, and you started the chorus as a sort of secondary act of kindness. Now the boys are dropping out and you're terribly hurt. Even your pride suffers for you must often have pictured how your little Drum and Fife Corps would look marching smartly along, with you the spirit of it all. But, John, think what you are still accomplishing."

"Such as what?"

"The chorus! Those girls are probably getting their first taste of a certain kind of beauty. And they may need it much more than the boys. Don't you dare belittle it."

Her eyes were very bright but there was a firmness to her lips which startled him.

"Touché," he said softly. "You hit me right in the solar plexus, but I certainly thank you. I'm still disappointed to death but it's true there was a lot of plain old vanity mixed up in my thinking. Now I'll concentrate better on the chorus. As soon as you can manage it, I'd like you to come down some afternoon and give a little help with the piano. The girls will love that."

He left early. "It's my emotions that are worn out," he said quaintly.

Hester stood, looking up at him. "And I only made it all worse, I fear. Oh, John, I do so sympathize with you. I can't bear for you to be hurt."

He bent closer to see her face. "Are those tears in your eyes? They surely couldn't be for me."

"Would you mind if they were?"

"Mind," he said wonderingly. He took out his handkerchief and very gently wiped them away. "I'm not worth those precious drops, Hester, but I can tell you they've comforted my heart. And now, I'd better go before I say what I shouldn't at the moment. But thank you — for everything."

He left quickly and Hester stood, trembling, amazed at the force of her own feeling. For never before had she known love, strong, rapturous in quality, passionate in potential. Certainly not in her marriage. She had not been aware then that such a feeling existed. Now she not only knew, she was experiencing it. But it was a tumultuous secret to be hidden and restrained, gloried in, perhaps, because she was sure John Justin felt the same and was for some reason exercising perhaps even stronger restraint. But why? What held him back? What in his past life made him afraid to speak the magic word itself, when his every look and action failed to conceal its verity in his heart?

At last she gathered Flushie into her arms, felt his soft, warm little body relax in contentment against her and went up to her room. But once in bed, her thoughts turned to the boys of Sackville, the dreamed-of Drum and Fife Corps. Justin, she knew, would not urge them or plead for the fulfillment of the plan. The willingness must come from the boys themselves. She tossed and turned and at times lay perfectly still, thinking of the situation from every angle. "They've got to *want* to practice," she kept saying aloud over and over. Then suddenly, when darkness was nearly over, she sat straight up against her pillows, sending Flushie from the foot of the bed to find the reason for her new position.

"I believe I've got it," she said. "At least it's worth a try and it really might work." And following this, she sank at once into sleep.

The chorus improved amazingly through the following weeks. With Hester's skillful accompaniment, the voices became stronger and more true. The harmony developed as though the young singers felt the whole mood of the song closing in upon them, drawing them together. Justin had bought some cheap little song books of which they were inordinately proud. They made many suggestions, some of which Justin followed, but it was soon clear that there was one general favorite: this was the "Londonderry Air."

Would God I were a tender apple blossom!

At first, Justin was hard put to it to keep his lips from twitching at the incongruities involved, but as the work continued he had a different feeling. These shabby Sackville girls in their cheap dresses had somehow caught the tender poignancy of the words better than he himself had ever done. So they begged to practice it over and over. The would-be altos sang while the sopranos hummed the tune; then they alternated. The first day Hester was at the piano they tried it all together, softly, to gain assurance and then with full accompaniment and what amounted to a burst of melody, they sang. And as they did, a strange thing occurred outside the tall windows from whence the jeers and ribald calls had been wont to come. The thing that happened now was silence.

At first, Justin, conditioned as he had been to the outside noises, was incredulous. He had even prepared Hester for what she might have to hear and still maintain her poise. But now, although he had been conscious of the scuffle of feet as usual below, and the first giggles and whispers which had before preceded the raucous calls, there was now no sound whatever. It was warm Indian summer and Justin felt the windows had to be raised for comfort, but he was afraid for Hester's sake. He need not have been. The much maligned chorus, singing their hearts out now in the song they loved, had somehow gotten through to the boys. They were listening.

When the last tender phrase had died on the air, there came a voice. It sounded like Bony's.

"Ain't half bad. Sing 'er again."

Justin, standing near the window, completely ignored the voice, or the possibility of anyone waiting below.

"That was fine, girls, but I believe I'd like to have you do it once more. Mrs. Carr will play the introduction, then take it a little more slowly and speak every word distinctly. Ready?"

The second rendition was even better than the first. The girls were more sure of themselves in any case, but the listening silence of the boys, ending in a real encomium, sent a thrill through them which nothing else could. Hester came from the piano to greet them warmly. "That was beautiful, girls. I never expected such singing. Now, I'll come to your rehearsals as often as ever I can. Do you feel the accompaniment helps?"

There were cries of pleasure. The girls' eyes devoured the finely tailored yellow suit Hester was wearing because Justin liked it and mentally decided to copy her hair style and make-up as nearly as they could. There was no practice on a new song, for Justin announced that the first glory must not be dimmed. They would grub along with some hard spots at their next rehearsal. He praised them with real feeling and watched their happy faces as they left. Then he and Hester walked slowly over the hill and along the Avenue until they reached her street.

"Didn't I tell you?" she said, at last. "Why, John, you've really performed a miracle. How can you let yourself be so disappointed over the boys' defection when you've achieved something as truly lovely as that chorus. And why did you warn me about the boys? They were as still as mice — if they were there at all."

Justin laughed. "They were there all right and the fact that they were quiet meant as much to me as the girls' singing. It was the bigger miracle of the two, really. Hope rises so easily in me — springs eternal, as Mr. Pope said. I just wonder if there still may be a way to — "

"I think this is the very night to tell you my idea. You're staying to dinner?"

"Yes, unless I bludgeon Hattie. She says she wants to hear about how the girls got on and to hear it from me, for you never tell her all the *dee*tails. Do you mean you really have been keeping something from me?"

"I had to, for a little while. It may be of no value, but I think it's worth a trial. Just after the girls' success might be the right time. You remember the night you were so terribly let down and ready to give the whole thing up?"

"I do, indeed."

"I couldn't sleep that night."

"Neither could I, but it was my problem, not yours. You must never lie awake worrying about me. I absolutely forbid it." He was quite stern.

Hester laughed gleefully. "And just how would you go about preventing me? Better practice first on easy things like stopping the wind from blowing, for instance. In any case, that night I had a sudden brainstorm, lightning flash or something that hit me violently. Please don't feel too confident. It may all be utterly useless. But since it's concrete in a way, I'll tell you and *show* you, after dinner."

"*Show* me!" he repeated, mystified.

"Yes, and I'll make a confession. I don't believe I could have held out even one more day without sharing the whole idea with you."

Dinner was exuberant. Hester let Justin give the full report to Hattie, even going into the kind of remarks (expurgated) which the boys had made previously. When he gave the favorite quatrain, Hattie was so overcome with mirth that she had to repair to the kitchen. She later appeared in the doorway. "Did you find out who any of them girls was?"

"Oh," Hester broke in, "there's a tall, rather pretty one with the second sopranos, her voice is almost an alto — but I swear she has perfect pitch and a lovely tone quality. Have you noticed?"

"Oh yes, from the first. She carries that whole end of the group. I think," he said hesitatingly, "she's the daughter of Liz, the woman you once described, Hattie."

"Her!" Hattie said aghast. "Now, Mr. Justin, you just watch your step when you go in there to see about the chorus or anything. That woman's *dangerous.*"

Justin, with a side glance at Hester's face, averted, answered gravely. "Thanks for your good advice, Hattie, but while I may not look it, I am perfectly able to take care of myself."

"Well, no harm in warnin' you again. An' I'm glad the singin' went so good."

When she was gone, Hester looked up, surprised. "The daughter of Liz. Of all strange things. Yet, as I remember now, Ginny told me that once when Lena Gibbs was going to have a big dinner party, she wanted to borrow some extra silver and Ginny took it over and heard this amazing voice coming from the kitchen where Liz was helping. It lasted only a few minutes and Lena didn't make much of it, but Ginny knows music and she said she got a thrill. There's a talent somewhere there."

"I'm sure of it. But let's forget it at the moment and tell me your idea. I can't stand this suspense."

"All right. We've both finished dessert. You go into the living room and wait while I bring it down."

"So! The idea is transportable!"

Hester only laughed. But in a short time she returned with a large suit box. She opened it and, from layers of tissue paper, drew out and laid across the sofa a perfect cadet suit. There was the tight-fitting little jacket with brass buttons, the pants with their white stripes down the sides and, topping it, a round hat of the same material, trimmed with gold braid and a tuft of white.

"There," she said. "There's your Drum and Fife Corps outfit. What do you think, Justin?"

His face was a study, at first it was evident he couldn't speak, but at last, in a husky tone, he said, "It's incredible and so are you. What can I say to you? Except what I don't dare," he added under his breath. "I can see your whole idea plainly. We have no way of knowing whether it will work or not, but it's the first gleam of hope that has come to me. Where did you ever get the suit?"

"We made it, Ginny and I, with the help of the village tailor. We found a pattern — don't ask me how — and we had fun doing it. The other girls have heard about it and they're all crazy to join the sewing circle — if they're needed."

"I hope to God they will be," Justin muttered.

"I'll pack it up again in its box," Hester said, "and you can take it up to school tomorrow morning and be casually showing it to Brown when the boys come in. Just a matter of interest in what *might* have been, you see?"

Justin nodded. "I see too much," he said, "and if you'll

forgive me for saying so little of all I feel, I think I will go on home."

She smiled and handed him the precious box. "Now, if it doesn't work don't be too disappointed. It's just a chance. And oh, I meant to say that after what the girls did this afternoon, they must have choir robes whether the boys get interested again or not. The robes would be dead easy to make and in a pretty color with white facings, they would love them, don't you think?"

Justin's eyes were wet. "Don't be so unspeakably kind, Hester. It gives me sort of a pain in my heart, for fear someday you might feel I'm not worth it."

"As if I ever could. You know what's wrong with you? You've had too much tension in a short time. You go home and have a hot toddy and go to bed. And don't say silly things to me. After all, we did this for the boys, not for you."

Justin managed a shaky laugh. "Now I deserved that. But I'll still claim a few little thoughts for myself. In any case, it was a stroke of genius and I was so dumfounded I couldn't half tell you so. I say it now and all my thanks. We'll hope for what tomorrow may bring."

"You'll tell me right away?"

"As if I could wait."

While he did not expect to relax so easily, Justin fell asleep at once after his hot drink and was ready early in the morning to go up to the Big Room for the great Test Case. As he passed the older boys in the yard, they eyed his box curiously and, as always, since their defection, had the grace to look abashed.

"Hi!" Justin called cheerfully.

They returned his greeting and then Bony said abruptly, "What you got in the box?"

"Oh, just a suit."

"For Brown?"

"No. Just thought he might like to see it." And he moved on.

Once in the Big Room, he told Brown quickly of the parts they were to play, then spread the suit, size fourteen, as Hester had explained, across the front desk. In a very short time the boys came noisily up the stairs, then crowded at the back of the room, their mouths agape as they looked.

"What's that for?" 'Loyshus, grandson of Snecky, asked quickly.

"Oh," Justin tried to say casually, "it's a Drum and Fife Corps suit which I thought Mr. Brown would like to see."

"Whatcha' goin' to do with it?" There was tension in Bony's voice.

"Well," Justin explained, "my plan was to have one of these for each of you if you had kept on until you learned your — *instruments* — " He smothered a faint smile here. "But now, since you've given it all up, I suppose I'll just— "

Bony's voice rose violently. "Who said we was givin' it all up? Honest, Mr. Justin, we was just foolin' an' we *was* mad at the way Snecky was ridin' us about the drums. But I tell you now an' I mean all you guys," he added, looking at his followers, "I'm goin' to wear one of them there suits if I have to work like hell to get it."

"Why don't you try this one on?" Justin asked calmly.

"It's just about your size. If you all decide to go ahead with the plan, we'll have the other suits made to measure. Come on, try this one."

Bony made a quick spring to the front desk, took suit and cap carefully in his arms and retired to the cloakroom. The girls were all in their seats now, so there was a full audience to see Bony as he came forth, martially arrayed. There was a second's silence while they all took in the miracle and then a wild burst of applause. Bony was, indeed, transformed. His stooping shoulders had straightened under the jacket pads; his whole body, indeed, seemed to have filled out; but most conspicuous was the fact that his head was now held high and his freckled face set in an expression of assurance, one might even say, dignity. He walked up and down the center aisle while the clapping and whistles of his peers continued. Then as Justin approached with a broad smile and shook hands, Bony made something that actually resembled a small bow before he left to don his usual wear.

When he returned Justin said, "Well, how about it, boys? Do you want to start in again and really work?"

"We sure do," they chorused.

"I'll speak to Mr. Webb and ask him to be a little more patient with you. You heard for yourselves what the girls have accomplished by steady work."

The boys looked sheepish. "They ain't half bad," Bony admitted.

"We'll get the drums out and I'll bring the fifettes when we set our next rehearsal. We're still missing one recorder."

"I know who's got it!"

"Shut your dirty mouth," yelled 'Loyshus promptly.

"It's him," the boys yelled. "He kep' it an' he can play a tune."

"Yotta' hear him."

"Do you have it here?" Justin asked.

"Sure! It's in his desk. I seen it!"

"How do you know so damned much about my business?" 'Loyshus countered.

"That's enough," said Mr. Brown. "No profanity in the schoolroom."

"Give us a tune, 'Loyshus, won't you?" Justin asked as if the routine was the most normal in the world.

The boy ducked his head, muttering darkly, felt through the papers and apparent miscellany in his desk and came up at last with the missing recorder.

"Ain't nothin'," he said, "I just picked out a song or two."

He stood, as though that position was essential, and like a young Pan put his lips to his rustic flute. And the sound came, clear and incredibly pure, filling the dusty schoolroom. It was something the boy had made up himself, Justin thought, for it seemed to have neither end nor beginning, but went melodiously on with now and then a minor which 'Loyshus blew slowly and softly. He stopped abruptly and handed the recorder to Justin.

"I wasn't *stealin'* it," he said. "I just kep' it to practice up on sometimes. Here 'tis."

Justin waved it back. "You've made good use of it, 'Loyshus. What you played was a lovely thing. You keep on practicing and you can be a big help to the others." He looked over the room. "I can confess to you now that I was pretty disappointed when you boys gave up on our plans, but now I'm happier than I can tell you. I'll keep the suit until you get on a little more with the work and then we'll take measurements for you all for a good fit. Meanwhile, we'll get the drums out and I'll bring the recorders and fifettes down as soon as we can arrange a practice. We'll try not to take up your time like this again, Mr. Brown."

The principal smiled. "I think I'm as pleased over this new turn of affairs as you and the boys are," he said.

That night, Hester gave a dinner party. When she had heard all the news and the way in which the suit had turned the tide, she said, her face shining, that this must be a celebration and it was high time now that Westbrook in general should know what was going on.

"It's certainly short notice but it's an off weekday night and everybody loves a party, so I'll get right on the phone and see what I can do. We ought to tell it all while it's hot."

The results were surprisingly good. There had been no parties for a week and the hidden excitement in Hester's voice sent waves of conjecture from house to house.

"It looks like an engagement to me," Jack Laird said. This idea was freely discussed, but everyone noted that Ginny Masters kept saying it might be some other kind of surprise and she was the greatest romantic of them all. In any event, there were five acceptances, which insured twelve at the table. The grocer and butcher were called and cajoled, Hester cut the last flowers, made her famous sponge custard, sorted the napery and dusted, while Hattie, trying to grumble and yet in high feather, rattled pans in the kitchen and told Flushie to keep from underfoot — a sure sign she was excited.

When John called up in the afternoon, Hester glowed over her report. "Three of our closest couple friends are coming and two others you don't know well, but whom I want to impress. They always take a dismal view of Sackville and I want to change it if possible."

"Could I come early and help?" he asked.

"No, thank you. Just come in at seven with the rest, only John, *please* bring your violin. I want them to hear my prize pupil if I dare call you that."

"That fits all right, but even if it didn't, you could call me anything you like and in my present state of euphoria I'd be sure to answer. Keep the fiddle in the background, though, *please.*"

At seven, the guests came, eager, it seemed, to find out the reason for the sudden party. There was an unusual amount of gaiety as drinks were served and quips of all sorts exchanged.

"There's something in this room that smells like romance," Bill Quinn finally pronounced, while the others hinted with delight, if less assurance. Hester was out of the room for the moment, but Justin was calmly ready.

"I swear you're right," he said with a grin, "and I think I know what it is. Hester says Hattie is entertaining an old widower every now and then in the kitchen."

Everyone laughed and the thin ice had been safely crossed. Hester reappeared and said Hattie was ready to serve dinner, so there was a reseating around the dining table in the candlelight. Hester had, for her own reasons, kept Bill Quinn next to her on one side with Tom Masters on the other. Justin was well placed also, she felt, between a warm friend and a possible foe to their plans. She had decided before to divulge their whole plan early in the meal, so there would be plenty of time for discussion later. When Hattie had removed the first course, Hester looked brightly around the table.

"You must have wondered why this sudden impulse to have a party. It was because I couldn't wait a minute longer to tell you all a wonderful secret which — "

There were wild outcries. "We knew it! We guessed it! Plain as the nose on your face! Our very best — "

"Let her finish," Justin called above the uproar.

"It has to do with Sackville!" Hester brought out quickly. All but Ginny looked deflated and even a bit resentful.

"You'll have to make a pretty good explanation of that," Bill Quinn said stiffly.

"We will," Hester said, "and though it's hardly fair to make him stop his dinner, I'm going to ask John to tell the whole story. Hattie will keep your food warm, by the way. Go ahead, John, and start at the beginning."

So he did. His voice was quiet, but because of his fine diction and eloquence of expression, the emotion came through. He had a gift for speaking and he drew upon all of it now. The guests around the table laughed and listened and wiped their eyes, laughed again or grew intense and serious, as Justin brought all the characters of his story to life in the unfolding of the little drama.

"So now," he ended, "we have Hester and Ginny to thank for the fact that the great scheme is going to work. For this time, I feel it won't fail. Well, how does it strike you all?"

"Oh, tell us again about the Girls' Chorus and the way

the boys acted. That was so funny and so touching too," Millie Laird urged.

But Bill Quinn raised his hand and asked to be heard. "Now before we all get too excited over this, there are a few things to say. I appreciate, Justin, your altruism, but remember, you are new to the town and may not know the whole situation. Sackville, if I may say so, is just a little too damned close to us as it is, and we certainly don't want to bring it any closer. It's a dirty little hole and our own doctor feels that for sanitary reasons the less we come in contact with it, the better."

The faces of the table guests wore expressions varying from resentment to agreement.

"And we all know the people there aren't honest. I've lost more good tools over the years by having various men work on the lawn. And I think the women have missed a few things now and then after dinner parties. On the whole, they're a bad lot and the less we get mixed up with them the better. Sorry to throw cold water on the scheme, Justin, but we have to be realistic about this thing."

There was an immediate buzz of voices, two of which said, "That's right, Bill. I'm with you about Sackville."

But the others were definitely on the other side. "Bill Quinn, I think you ought to be ashamed of yourself," Ginny spoke with her usual forthrightness. "Here we have the chance to do some good for once, and you're afraid of soiling your hands on something."

"That's right," Millie Laird said, still apparently moved by Justin's recital. "I think it's time we did something for the Sackville people and not just stick up our noses and pretend they aren't there. I'll help sew on the suits or the robes or anything. I can't understand you, Bill Quinn, and you a vestryman in the church and everything!"

By dessert most of the dissenters had been silenced or had changed their views of their own accord. The majority of the guests were in full cry after more details and Justin's face had regained some color after being stone white.

"I can't see why Westbrook would be more sullied by our scheme for the children then it already is by workmen and cleaning or serving women from Sackville," he said.

"Of course it wouldn't," Tom Masters spoke strongly. "That's ridiculous. Even if it were, I'd say we've got to go on with this for the good of our souls. We've been a pretty selfish lot if you come right down to it. For my part, I'm a little excited to see the thing get rolling. Does this mean we're to stop talking?" he asked as Hester rose.

"By no means." She smiled. "We'll go on harder than ever, I hope, with the open fire to stimulate us in the living room."

There were still pros and cons, and a few sharp questions. "What's to be the end of this if you really get your Drum and Fife Corps trained?" Bill Quinn asked.

"Now you've really asked a good one," Justin answered, "and I can't reply too concretely, for I don't know. But I have the idea that if they ever accomplish this thing they will have learned a little discipline and dignity and had a glimpse of a different kind of life; even a bit of beauty itself. And of course, they could play on every possible occasion. Can't you just see them entertaining the inhabitants of Sackville who would be sitting on their front steps?" He glanced at Hester. "Don't you think it's time now to display the suit?"

"I've just been waiting. Come on, Ginny. You were a partner in this."

In a few minutes, they came downstairs bearing the work of their hands . . . Ginny held it up against her as she was shorter and Hester put on her head the little cap. The effect on the group was almost as electrical as it had been on the boys.

"By Gad, that's good!" Jack Laird called out. "You go ahead, Millie, and help all you can with this business. Why that's the cleverest thing I ever saw for two gals to make!"

"We had a little help from the tailor, but not much," Ginny put in.

Bill Quinn was now all but in tears. "I just melt away at sight of that," he apologized. "You see, I had one just about like that first year they sent me away to school. Hated the school, but felt like a major-general in the suit. Well, Justin, maybe you've got an idea there after all," he said, blowing his nose.

The party was late in breaking up, but some things had been happily settled. A group for sewing had planned regular meetings and, more surprising still, the men had offered contributions to cover expenses of cloth, tailoring and some extra instruments. Justin stayed a little longer to talk it all over, but this was a usual custom. Tonight, Tom Masters, after he had reached his car, came running back.

"Listen, Justin, apropos of our Sackville neighbors, Bill Hoover was mending my garage door one day and he sort of snarled, 'I'll get him yet, I will: Teachin' our kids all that fool nonsense!' I just thought of it now. Has he got a grudge or doesn't he like the drum corps idea?"

"God knows," Justin said. "He's a queer one, but I'll be at pains to pacify him. Thank you for telling me, Tom."

When they were back inside, Hester expressed her own anxiety. "They really are a bad lot. Do you think any of them could actually hurt you for interfering, as they might call it, with their children?"

Justin tried to smile. "Oh, I'm sure, not in any physical way. They might hurl epithets at me or something of the kind. But I fancy the parents will be as proud over those suits as the boys. By the way, tonight, in a different fashion, was a triumph. We've got a real nucleus of interest started now. Even Quinn, who was bristling for battle at first, melted completely when he saw the suit! You're wonderful, Hester! I can't ever thank you enough. But on top of everything else, I enjoyed the fine evening and the way things are lining up. I didn't tell you, but the boys are going back into practice tomorrow. I talked it all over with Snecky and he's promised to tone down his criticisms and give the kids some praise. He was really quite upset when he heard they were thinking of giving up. By the way, this boy, this 'Loyshus, I find, is a son of Liz, so he comes honestly by his musical talent. And he's got it, all right, like the girl in the chorus."

"Have you ever seen Liz?"

"No, but I'd like to."

Hester laughed. "You'd better not. Hattie *would* have a story then!"

"Wouldn't she? Well, needless to say, what I want is to

find out if I can where all this music comes from. Old Snecky says she's his daughter, but somehow, I don't believe it. There's no resemblance, and besides, I think he's too old. The pieces just don't fit. But if she has a mystery she doesn't intend to broadcast it. She keeps out of my way, that's sure, and I don't believe Westbrook has found out any facts about her, either, have they?"

"Nothing except the glaring one which Hattie explained to you with such relish," Hester said with a small laugh. "But, forgetting Liz for the moment, I'm so glad Snecky is going to encourage the young drummers, and of course you will carry the fifers right along. Oh, I'm so terribly glad everything is beginning again. I have a good sewing group lined up and I think we should start soon on some more suits. If the boys see several others completed it will keep the enthusiasm high. Could you begin to measure them? Give us the ages, for I hope we can get patterns, but give us also, for each one, the length of sleeve and jacket and pant leg. Could you do this soon, John, and we'll start?"

"Angel of Sackville!" he said.

As they stood in the hall before he left, Hester looked up at him with a troubled face. "You managed to avoid playing your violin — also I still feel worried about what Bill Hoover said to Tom. You don't really think you are in any danger?"

"Nonsense," Justin tried to say stoutly, "the only way they could hurt me would be with words."

"But I don't want to see you hurt at all," Hester said, very low.

CHAPTER FIVE

DURING THE NEXT WEEKS several strange things happened. Westbrook roused from its comfortable social lethargy and felt a new interest stirring in the conversations of the commuters, the bridge players, the groups of women chatting over late morning coffee and the Saturday golfers around the clubhouse. The subject, of course, was Sackville and whether its sudden emergence upon the scene was a good thing or not. At least it was a live and interesting topic and there were many citizens who felt much more deeply and looked off frequently over the low bordering hill, thinking for the first time of their neighbors. There were even a few men who, under cover of darkness, had made their quiet way to the back door of the house of Liz, when they were supposed to be at a meeting. These few thought most deeply of all.

The drum and fife practice had begun, this time not with excitement or exhilaration, but with a dogged, determined, do-or-die attitude which Justin knew would bring results. Three more cadet suits were already in the making, he made sure to tell the boys.

One of the unlikely things that took place during those late fall days was the beginning of a friendship between old Snecky Webb, the drummer, and Justin himself. It started like a tiny green shoot from the ground, scarcely visible, but, little by little, it grew until there was form and substance. It had begun when Justin explained to Snecky that the boys were quitting their practice partly from discouragement. Could he give them a little praise if they started again? Not so much criticism perhaps?

The effect on Snecky was startling. Weak tears began to run down his cheeks to such a degree that Justin offered his own fresh handkerchief since the old man apparently had none. Snecky touched the clean linen, smoothed it and held it for a few moments, almost tenderly, against his face. Then he said chokingly, "I was so goldarned proud, I guess, to be teachin' them, an' one or two was really gettin' the hang of it wonderful. I s'pose I was rough on them just because I never had a chance to show off any way before."

He mopped his eyes with the handkerchief again and then returned it. "I was all set up about the idea of the boys learnin' the drum and then to think I spoilt everything. But I'll tell you what, Mr. Justin, if you can get them to come back to it, I'll make it up to them, so I will. I'll teach them all I know, but I'll be good to them, you know, I won't be always yammering at them. Can you get them back?"

"I think so."

"Well, thank God for that. I'll get another chance, then. Stay a little while, Mr. Justin. Liz, she's up helpin' some woman in Westbrook. She ain't strong, but she can shine up the silver an' do little fancy things some of the other women here can't. I'd like to tell you about Liz, that is, if you'd care to hear."

"I would like to, very much."

"Well, see, it's like this. I always call her my daughter for it's easiest to say, but she ain't any relation to me, reely. She's the daughter of a buddy of mine. He was a widow man an' I was a bachelor an' we just kinda' stuck together. He had this daughter Liz, an' glory, but she was pretty, an' always singin' 'round the house. My buddy, he was full of music. He had a boy too, I mind, but he never paid much mind to his kids. He was always busy savin' up his money to buy a fiddle, or 'damme,' he'd say, he might even get one of them there parlor organs."

Snecky stopped for breath and Justin said in a strange voice, "Go on."

"We both worked at a little private coal mine two farms over an' we made out pretty well an' then everything went sour. Liz got into trouble twice over an' was sort of sickly like after 'Loyshus was born. Her pap was clean furious an' said he'd throw her an' her brats out, he said. He was a high-tempered cuss an' poor Liz had nowhere to go an' I told her I had room and she could come here. So she came. I was sorry for her for I felt Bill Hoover had been 'round her an' she couldn't stand him. Well, that split things up between my buddy and I an' then the slate fell in the mine an' near to broke my back an' I couldn't work no more. So we used up all my savings. I hadn't been too careful with them, not like my buddy, but *he* wouldn't help us one bit, an' what was we to do? This is what I want to ask you, Mr. Justin, for people speak awful hard of Liz."

There was a little silence and then Snecky broke it. "As I told you, she wasn't strong after 'Loyshus like the other women to stretch carpets an' beat rugs an' wash an' iron an' all that. She just had one way, seemed like, that she could earn a little money to keep our bodies an' souls together an' that's what she done. It wasn't much I'll tell you except once in a while, but she was a good manager and somehow, with little bits of work for the women on the side, we got enough to eat. What I wanted to ask you, Mr. Justin, do you blame her for doin' all she knowed to do after I took her in an' give her a home?"

"She didn't *want* to do this?"

"Never! I've seen her cry something awful many a night."

"Then I think she has been a brave woman."

Snecky drew a long breath. "I thank you. You've eased my heart. I wished you could speak to her an' just tell her that Vi'let and' 'Loyshus are doin' good with their music. It would please her. She's kind to me an' she's a good mother, Liz is, but she's special tender to 'Loyshus. So that's all. Mr. Justin?"

"Yes, Mr. Webb."

"It's sort of helped me to talk this all out with you. Could you stop in again an' see me?"

"I'd be glad to."

"I sit here so much for I can't walk without my crutches,

you know, an' I think about all sorts of things an' I ain't got anyone to talk it all out with. If you'd just listen sometimes — "

"It might help me too, you never know."

He had barely spoken the words when suddenly, the back door flew open and a woman entered. Justin could not see her face.

"Come on in, Liz. I got a caller. Mr. Justin's here, an' he says your kids are doin' fine with their music."

"They are indeed." Justin spoke as the woman, Liz, made no move to come into the room. "You should be proud of them. I think they both have real talent, especially 'Loyshus."

"Thank you," she answered in a low voice as though much moved, then added, "Dad, I have to go right back."

"I'm sorry not to have met her," Justin said, as the door could be heard closing.

"Yes, I don't know what the hurry was, but she's awful shy. Doesn't make too many friends 'round here. But she's heard of you often enough from the kids. You said just the right thing an' I knowed she'd be pleased. Now if you call in again to see me, she won't be so scared." Snecky sighed. "She's still pretty, but not like she was," he added.

"She's probably still a fine-looking woman," Justin said. "Of course, time changes us all. Well, good-bye, Mr. Webb. I'll be seeing you soon and I enjoyed the call."

That night he told Hester of his near encounter with Liz. "I'm puzzled," he said. "There's something vaguely familiar about her voice and yet, she's an utter stranger. I keep wondering — "

"John," Hester said, laughing reproachfully, "it really

isn't quite proper for you to go 'round thinking of Liz all the time."

He laughed then too and took her hand in his. "There's just one woman whom I'm really interested in thinking about. This business of Liz is like a puzzle. I can't make the pieces fit. I'll have to take my chances, though, in dropping in to see Snecky when I can. He's a nice old soul and terribly lonely. I don't think Lib will bother us."

"What did you call her?"

"I don't know. What do you mean?"

"You called her *Lib.*"

"Oh," he said, "just a slip of the tongue, I guess. Lib and Liz are a good deal alike. Well now, tell me the latest news of the sewing circle. Those boys are working their heads off now to get a suit."

"Good! We have two more finished, two more well on the way and two cut out! The girls are so funny. They keep saying this is much more fun than sewing for *missions,* for now we can see the work of our hands on parade. Have you thought, John, of any sort of entertainment you can have them give when they are all trained and rigged out? In other words, what event could it all be leading up to?"

"You're psychic," he pronounced, "for I was going to consult with you tonight about an idea. It's a pretty big one and the air could go out of the balloon completely, but I'm dying to talk about it, so here goes."

"Put another log on the fire, first, and then we can really settle. The nights are getting cool."

When the blaze flared, they sat facing it, each expectant, with Flushie, as usual, between. "It is a big, presumptuous idea and I haven't too much hope, but why not try? It's like this. We must have some sort of a 'do' when the children are ready to perform and of course we can just have a performance in the Big Room itself, but when all the performers get in, there won't be much room for an audience. Another thing — "

Justin looked nervous but went on. "If they do as well as I think now they will, I would certainly like to have some Westbrook citizens see the small miracle along with Sackville. If ever the twain could meet," he added, ruefully. "So!"

"You're still hedging," Hester said. "Please tell the big idea at once. I can't bear to wait longer."

"It's simply this. Or better to say, complicatedly this. I would like to begin putting out feelers toward a Christmas concert and tableau sort of thing in the Westbrook Junior High School Auditorium, given by the youth of Sackville, or even in that of the High School itself. Am I crazy?"

Hester watched him and for a second said nothing. Then, "I think it's the craziest and most beautiful idea I ever heard! It's so incredible that in fact it just might work. Have you begun putting out your feelers yet?"

"In a way. Brown, as you know, is doing a good job. In the evenings he often hobnobs with the Westbrook Junior High math teacher who in turn is friendly with the High School principal. So there's a contact. Then, Tom Masters is on the school board and I'm sure he would back the project. I've only mentioned a few generalities to him, but I'll come down to real information later. And questions. But you really think it might all have a chance? I know you'll be honest."

Hester's answer was, at first, oblique. "Ginny, of course,

has heard the chorus and she's most terribly impressed. We might let the whole sewing group in on one of their rehearsals. I believe after that you would have a line of enthusiasts to bolster up the plan. And, yes, John, I do honestly believe it might work out. If so, oh heavenly day! What a triumph! But there will be objections aplenty and all sorts of hurdles to overcome. Of course, you know that all too well. But by the same token, what a challenge! Your eyes are sparkling already!"

"So are yours," he said. "From the two of us, the idea ought to catch on." He leaned forward, watched the burning wood. "I believe I'll tell you a little of what has gone behind all this. If — if you'd care to hear?"

She smiled. "As if you needed to ask that."

"Well, I'll try to be brief. This early summer, I suddenly one day ran into a full-length mirror in the new dormitory. Of course, what I saw was the *physical* me, but more, I somehow perceived the man inside my skin and I didn't like him. I went back to my room to think it over and I saw my life in review. First I was a carefree, then a serious, student, then a bachelor college professor interested in my work, social enough, without being convivial, but through it all, absolutely selfish, completely self-centered. I decided to take my sabbatical at the end of the college year and come here since I had heard of Westbrook as a quiet, suburban town, to get a more objective view of my life."

"But I begin to see," Hester said triumphantly. "You told me almost at once that you were coming here to pay a long-due debt. You meant a debt to humanity, didn't you?"

"You could put it under that general heading, I guess. Well, during my nightly walks which I took in order to be alone with myself under the stars, I reconstructed my life. My first emergence from my shell was in the direction of Sackville. I guess you can take it on from there. But I still deeply regret my lost, selfish years."

"Perhaps we would all do the same if we were as honest as you," Hester said thoughtfully. "As I look upon it, my own life seems pointless and, oh dear, too comfortable and smug and selfish. As a matter of fact, most of Westbrook is the same. We go through the prescribed ritual. We women belong to the Altar Guild, and the sewing groups for good causes; the men, many of them, serve as vestrymen from time to time, but none of this goes very deep. Take Sackville for an example. All over the years, nobody thought about it or did anything for it, until you opened our eyes. Our one idea was to keep it as far away as possible."

"Oh please, don't reproach yourself because of what I said, I couldn't stand that. You've lived a full life, your circumstances were so different. In my own case — "

He was interrupted by the sharp clang of the knocker. Flushie leaped from his place on the sofa and ran barking to the door with Hester close upon his heels. When she opened it, Bill Quinn, his face flushed and angry, pushed past her to where he could see Justin in the hallway.

"I told you," he shouted, "I told you we'd have trouble getting mixed up with Sackville. And now it's *come* to *me* and I tell you that I want the whole thing stopped!"

"Come in," Hester said placatingly. "Come in and tell us what the matter is."

"I'll stand right here, Justin, and say my say to you. It's you that's stirred up all the trouble. My daughter Melissa and a friend of hers walked back to the Village Row this evening. This boy from Sackville was working there at this little hamburger and soda place where our High School kids go and he had the gall, the effrontery, to walk my daughter, *Melissa,* home! *My* child! With a Sackville boy. It's monstrous and I tell you, I want the whole thing stopped. What have you to say for yourself, Justin?"

Justin's face had paled during the harangue, but his voice was calm.

"How did you know this?"

"I saw them coming up our walk. I was on the porch. I faced them and told that boy to go back where he belonged and never bother Melissa again. I sent her to her room. What are you going to do about this?"

"Well, first of all, nothing I have done with the younger children had anything to do with this boy's getting a job. He probably had it before I ever came. I don't know him, but Melissa has probably known him for some time since she and her friends often go there. Teen-agers always have a special place where they get together. She must feel he's a nice boy. I don't think you should have been so harsh."

Quinn simply stared at the man before him. "Harsh!" he brought out at last. "Faced with a situation like that, what would *you* do? Maybe my daughter's honor is in jeopardy if she sees this boy again. *Harsh!* I should have collared him and thrown him off my lawn."

"Easy," Justin said. "You forget you're dealing with very volatile material when you attack young people. I think you should say nothing more to your daughter. The more you rant against this boy, the more she'll want to see him. But I'll tell you what I'll do at once. I'll find out all I can about him. What's his name?"

"Oh, I think she called him *Mac.* She even said good-bye to him, after all I told him."

Suddenly he wilted and sat down heavily in the hall chair. "This has laid me low. Melissa's all we have. She's the apple of my eye. We've tried to be so careful of her. Now, God help me, I'm *scared.*"

"That's foolish," Justin said. "I've seen Melissa. She looks like a girl of uncommonly good sense. Aren't you really making a mountain out of a molehill? All teen-agers meet and often make sudden friendships that hardly last a month. Try to get a perspective on this. Did you see anything unusual as they came up your walk?"

"Yes, I did. They weren't talking and laughing, they were just looking at each other and they were *holding hands.*"

"That's not a crime," Justin tried to say lightly. "It's quite natural. Now, you try to get hold of yourself and consider this all a small episode. Also, act as usual with your daughter. She may be very angry and edgy tomorrow morning. You be gentle and, if necessary, say you were startled tonight or wouldn't have spoken so loud. On my part, I'll find out all I can about the boy. It may all be good enough that you'll have no fear, at any rate. Hester's the soul of hospitality as you know, but I'd advise you now to go right home and go to bed."

"Does your wife know of this?" Hester asked.

"Not yet. She was out at a board meeting."

"Wait till morning then, unless you feel she would take this matter more lightly than you."

"Afraid not. But I will go along home. I'm sorry I blustered so, but I still feel distraught."

"Don't apologize. I know everything will straighten out," Justin said as Quinn left.

When he had gone, Hester and John looked at each other in dismay.

"I never counted upon running into anything like this," Hester said with a burdened sigh.

"Nor did I. In spite of my brave talk, I'm scared too. In a word, I'm terrified, first, because I don't like the boy-and-girl setup and then, because it might — I can't think it will — but it might disrupt all our plans, everything we've dreamed of as the boys and girls practice. And they're doing *so* well now."

"We'll go right along with our plans, then?"

"Absolutely. We won't give ground until there's some sort of showdown. I hope to heaven it won't come."

As he said good night, he pressed his lips to Hester's hair. "My dear, my dear," he said, "be patient with me, I have problems too."

The first fall wind blew that night, a haunting sound with the moan of coming winter in it. As he lay sleepless, Justin heard the scurry of leaves blown here and there by the force lying in wait for them, even now making its power felt against their frailty. Yet, Justin thought, the brightness in the summer trees had seemed so invulnerable, so invincible, so *eternal.*

The wind died down after midnight; Justin rose and

looked out the window into the moonlight. There they were: the scarlet and gold which had lifted their colors in gay assurance to the hot midday suns, lying now, prostrate, stricken, on lawn and walk and street. And they were but the beginning. Steadily borne by the mood of the wind, others would follow! All would go, until there would be left only "the bare ruined choirs" where late the birds had sung.

It was a feeling of inner desolation which overtook him as he thought of his own life, his great love and the barrier made more acute by this night's disclosures and the problem of a Sackville boy and a Westbrook girl. For by some intuitive wisdom, he did not believe the interest between them which her father had witnessed had been the first. He finally fell into troubled sleep after deciding to talk to Snecky.

He found the old man the next morning, alert and eager to talk to him. He said they were alone in the house and asked if anything was the matter.

"You look sorta' worried, Mr. Justin. Ain't the kids doing so good? The drum boys are sure catchin' on to it. They've told me about the suits."

"I am worried, Mr. Webb, and I want your help. I know what I say you won't repeat to anyone."

"No fear of that."

"Well, it seems that a boy named Mac — "

"Yep. Mac Carson. He's Bony's older brother. What about him?"

"He's working at the little hamburger and Coke store back in Village Row. Last night he walked Melissa Quinn to her home, her father saw them and he's furious. He even blames me. What can I do? And what can you tell me about this boy?"

"He's a good lad. Never knew him to be in any trouble of any kind. Quiet sort. About the only one I know that had gumption enough to try to get a job back in the Row. The others always stuck around here and messed about pickin' up a few dollars and then finally wandered off, God knows where. They were always skittish about bein' among the Westbrook people, though of course they managed to pick up news."

"Do you suppose I could talk to Mac?"

"Don't see why not. He talks easy when he gets started. He lives in the fifth house up from here. Try it. But I tell you, he's a good lad. Wish you could stay longer here, but come back soon."

Justin found the house a little more neat in its front yard than most. Someone had evidently swept the leaves from the broken stone path. Justin crossed it, reached the door and knocked. There was silence at first in answer and then the sound of movements. At last the door opened and Justin saw before him a tall boy with handsome features and a pair of keen, gray eyes. He was in his bare feet and his thatch of brown hair had not been combed. He looked as though he had scrambled into a worn sweater and not-too-clean dungarees when he got out of bed.

"Yes?" he said.

"I'm John Justin and I come to you as a friend. Would you let me come in and talk with you for a few minutes?"

The boy nodded and opened the door wider. " 'Bout last night, I suppose." His tone was steel.

"Yes, it is," Justin answered. "But now I'm here I honestly don't know what to say."

"Well, you can fire any questions you want to at me. I've done nothing wrong."

"Mac, how long have you known Melissa?"

He flushed, but his eyes never flinched. " 'Bout a year, I guess. I've been workin' at that shop in the Row that long an' she's always comin' in with the other kids."

"This is a personal question, Mac, but have you noticed her specially?"

And then something dynamic came into the boy's face. Justin felt it as though a hot wave had passed through him. This boy had magnetism.

"Tell me about it, Mac. No matter what you say, it will be safe with me. I swear."

"Well," Mac began, still with the unflinching eyes. "It's been like this for a long time now. I could feel it when she came through the door and sat down at one of the little tables. I would look right at her then and she'd be lookin' at me an' her face would color up and I'd feel on fire. And this has been the way it was until last night."

"Why was last night different?"

"Well, you see, us Sackville fellahs keep to ourselves. We know we ain't welcome in Westbrook, but we get around, over at the Row an' here an' there an' we know the score. An' we all know Curly Huston is no good. I don't need to spell it out, Mr. Justin. He drives when he's drunk an' he ain't good for a girl to be with."

Here Mac stopped and swallowed with difficulty. "So, last night, when Melissa was sittin' with some kids, this

Curly come swaggerin' in half-stoned then — he can always get it somewhere — an' he went right up to Melissa an' begun sort of honeying around her an' I couldn't stand it. I took some fresh water to the table and leaned a little toward Melissa an' asked if I could walk her home. She looked up kind of surprised an' she sort of blushed an' then she said, 'Yes, you can.' Told her I might be a little late leaving, but to wait for me. An' she did." Mac's voice broke. "An' we walked sort of slow back an' talked about how we always felt each other was near, someway. Oh, it was a nice talk and we never stopped till we got to her house an' even then I forgot we was holdin' hands until her father lit out on us. You may not believe this, Mr. Justin."

"I certainly do believe you. I feel ashamed myself of the way Mr. Quinn spoke. The thing, Mac, is what to do next."

The boy drew a long heartbreaking sigh. "This life ain't fair," he said.

"That is true, in a sense, but it's up to us to make the best we can of it. I'd like to ask you one question. How long have you had a feeling of love for Melissa?"

The boy looked almost angry. "If anybody else had said that to me — " Then he stopped as though ashamed. "But I know you're tryin' to help me or you wouldn't be here. Just be sure to keep my secrets. I've loved Melissa last winter an' all this summer. All that time our eyes just met like I told you as though we was both on fire, but nothing else till last night."

"My dear boy," Justin said. "I don't know just what I can do. I'm afraid I can't ease your heart. I know something of love myself. But if you allow me, I'll talk to Mr.

Quinn and try to take away the bitterness of last night. Meanwhile, do your work, try to believe that things will straighten out, come to me for anything and God bless you."

He reached out his hand and Mac clasped it hard. Once again, Justin was conscious of a compelling strength in this boy. Coupled with the handsome face, the burning fire in his eyes when they met those of Melissa, he could imagine how the heart of a tender young girl would feel the magnetism and be drawn to him in her first longing.

He left the house, heavy-hearted. In all his fears and discouragements he had never counted upon anything like this. This was serious. This was not only the probable breaking of two young hearts, it would very possibly mean the disruption or end of all his hopes for his drum corps and chorus. Just how this would be accomplished he did not know, but the memory of a face, wild with anger, made him fear.

As he approached Hester's house, he saw her cutting the late chrysanthemums, with Flushie frisking jubilantly about among the flowers and the fallen leaves. She came over to the car at once as Justin got out.

"Any news?" she asked quietly.

"I had a talk with the boy. I'm sure he's good. I'm going to try to see Quinn tonight and give him what I found out. Then I'll stop in afterward and tell you how things went."

"You are anxious?"

"Very!"

They said nothing more and Hester went into the house. The dull morning turned into rain again. Flushie was restless when a thunderstorm broke and would not leave Hester's side. Hattie muttered constantly and cried out with each reverberation, sitting with her feet up on a chair.

"It's temptin' Providence to sit with your feet on the floor. Anybody knows the lightning could run right through them. You and Flushie get on the sofa and stay there! An' mind, you're mortal like everybody else. Get up now."

Hester, with poor Flushie shaking in every hair, obediently stretched out on the couch. She wondered if the last of the rain was making Justin's dark problem still darker. If the boy was decent and his only fault was that he came from Sackville, how could they possibly stop him from walking with Melissa? But they could. They would. Between Sackville and Westbrook a great gulf was fixed. The tears suddenly were hot in her eyes, for she felt pain not only for the young love threatened, but for her own. Justin still had not spoken. Would he ever?

The rain stopped about six, the thunder had spent itself and the lightning fires were put out. Instead, there spread over the sky a perfect glory of rose and turquoise clouds, not only across the west but, as though to atone for the ravening storm, even touching the north and east with color. Justin stood on his small porch considering the beauty following the terror of the elements. And he thought of the boy, of Mac. He thought of his eyes, honest, stern for a boy, with an unquenchable light in them as he spoke of Melissa. Justin's own heart ached with understanding for he too knew a great love that had a barrier.

After a bit of dinner which he had trouble swallowing, he dialed Quinn's number.

*

"Yes?" The voice was sharp. "This is John Justin. I would like to have a talk with you tonight if possible, either at your house or mine."

There was a brief pause and then the sharp voice answered. "I'll be over at your house at eight. And what you say to me had better be good."

When they were seated, together at last, Justin did not wait. "I saw the boy this morning — "

"And what did he have to say for himself?"

"He told me very simply how this matter that worries you came about."

"Let's hear it." There was irony in the tone.

Justin repeated as accurately as he could what Mac had said, omitting only the fact that he was in love with Melissa.

"And you believed this cock-and-bull story?"

"Absolutely, and if you would talk with him, so would you. He has the most honest eyes I've ever seen in anyone's head. How did Melissa seem today?"

"She won't talk. It breaks me all up. We've never been like this before. Her mother says, let things ride and it will all blow over. But somehow or other, as I looked at that boy — "

"I know what you mean."

"I'm afraid. There's something about him that could attract a girl. I'm terrified, the times being the way they are. We've tried to bring Melissa up so carefully, so safely. She's never really had a lot to do with boys and we were just as glad. And now to see her walking along holding hands with a *Sackville* boy — I don't know what to do."

"I agree with your wife. I think you are making too much of this. If I were you, I would act as usual with Melissa, maybe dropping a hint that there are some pretty nice boys in Westbrook, and just let the matter pass. All young folks have passing fancies for each other. As to this episode of last night, I think you should thank Mac for protecting Melissa. This other character, Curly, is, according to Mac, a devil-may-care driver, but the girls apparently think it's pretty smart to ride with him. I would say the danger lurks there and not with Mac. You should, I think, warn your daughter of this."

"If we had a big family, I suppose I'd be used to emotional jolts, but since Melissa is all we have — I can't get any perspective at all. Well, I'm sorry I snapped at the boy and then at you too. I'll try to get my bearings. You've been a great help and I thank you. I may be back for more advice."

"For what it's worth, it's all yours. And remember, for a boy and girl to walk along a path holding hands is not a serious offense." He smiled, but Quinn did not return it.

"A *Sackville* boy! That's the difference. And Justin, I'll count on you to somehow make it clear to this Mac, better even than I can, what the facts are."

He turned quickly and went out with a short good-night.

Justin followed him but took the opposite turning and soon found himself at Hester's home where the lights were still bright. Flushie greeted him with delighted barks and pulled him with a gentle tooth in his trouser leg to his usual seat on the couch, waited for Hester to sit down, then settled himself between them. These small antics broke the tension they both felt and they chatted a minute before Justin gave the account of the day.

When he finished Hester's eyes were wet. "Poor children!" she said. "What do you make of it? What can you do?"

Justin looked anxious and white. "If Quinn thinks I'm going to tell Mac he can't ever see Melissa because he's from Sackville, he's wrong. I won't do that. I'll try to see the boy as much as I can and drop an innuendo or two, but I won't spell it out in black and white. He's a smart boy. He knows without anyone's telling him in a way to break his spirit completely. Of course, I don't really know Melissa."

"I do," said Hester, "and she's just the kind to inspire a boy's first love, if he's sensitive to beauty. She's lovely really, looks as the Lady of Shalott might have looked. Serious and rather quiet until an enchanting smile breaks over her face. She's not the kind the average boy would rush to date, not the 'life of the party' kind, but something much deeper and sweeter. And unlikely as it seems, Mac has been the one to recognize it."

Justin drew a long breath. "The whole situation gets worse the more we consider it. And in the middle is Quinn himself, still angry and determined I'm to stop contacts with Sackville. Well, I can't do that, even though I feel this problem as any father might. The practices have never gone so well as just now. I've been having great hopes for the Christmas show." His face was set. "I'm not giving up on that until every resource is exhausted."

"By that time, I'm afraid *you'll* be," Hester said, a tenderness in her voice.

Through a long and particularly bleak November with

only small glimpses of real Indian summer breaking through the mists and occasional light snow showers, Justin tried his best to keep track of the young lovers. He found Mac reticent, though always friendly. He managed to see Melissa again as Hester pointed her out from a group. It was true. She was lovely in a delicate, almost ethereal way, though there was, as he looked and listened, a quick joyousness to her laugh. He haunted the narrow macadam paths, which the original architect, with unusual sensitivity, had run between the squares in which the town was laid out. Twice he saw Mac and Melissa walking slowly, hands clasped, unspeaking. Once, under an oak still canopied with leaves, he saw a long, breathtaking kiss! Even so, he asked himself, what could he do? What could anyone do in the face of the first sweet pangs of love, be it sprung from Sackville or Westbrook. Especially what could he say after looking into the boy's blazing eyes and having once lately seen the two pause for a moment in their walk as Melissa laid her head on his shoulder while his arm held her strongly to him. As he had urgently advised, Quinn said no more to Mac for the present, but made to Melissa a sort of joking apology which included him. But he made it clear to Justin that while patient for the moment, he would not let things go on much longer.

One Saturday morning, when Hester answered the phone, it was Melissa on the wire.

"Mrs. Carr?" The voice sounded husky but controlled. "I'm trying to make a dress and I need a little help with the pattern. Would you be at home any evening if I would go over?"

"Of course. I'll be here tonight. Could you come then?"

"Tonight?" There was a little catch in her breath. "Why, why, yes, I could come tonight. Maybe about eight?"

"That will be fine. I'll look for you. Though I'm no professional seamstress, you must remember." Hester smiled.

"Oh thanks," said the girl, but her voice quavered. "My mother will pick me up at nine."

"There's more to this than meets the eye," Hester murmured to herself and when Justin arrived just after lunch, he confirmed it.

What had happened was that he had gone to see Mac that morning, but almost before he could speak, the boy himself, his face white and stern, had given him the facts.

"Her old man — I mean Melissa's father — sent for me last night an' I went. He wasn't mad this time, but just sort of quiet like, he laid it on the line. I looked 'round the room we was in an' even if I hated him, I knowed he spoke the truth. I ain't right for Melissa. Then he went on to tell me how worried she was and couldn't eat or anything an' then — " He stopped and swallowed with difficulty.

"Then he asked me if for her sake I'd get the hell out of town right away. An' what could I say? I couldn't stay on an' see Melissa and not even touch her. I finally told him I'd go. To the city, I guess. He laid a lot of money on the table an' I pushed it right back to him. He ain't buyin' me off. He ain't got enough money for that if I thought we had a chance." He paused.

"We wanted a place we could be all alone to say goodbye an' we thought of Mrs. Carr. She's been so kind to the kids like you have. I seen Melissa an' she says we can go there tonight. I can't talk about it anymore. If you're there too and you an' Mrs. Carr can just leave us by ourselves a little while — "

Justin could only nod and put his arm around the boy's shoulder. "We'll arrange it," he said, his voice unsteady. "You're the bravest boy I know."

All afternoon, Justin spent at his typewriter, tearing sheet after sheet from the machine, for another he felt expressed better what he had to say. At last he let one stand: his praise, how empty; his encouragement, how barren; but also his most practical advice. Also, the addresses of three men he felt would see that Mac found some suitable lodgings and as days passed, a job of some sort, any sort. In the envelope he enclosed some bills and then sealed it. On the outside he printed: KEEP THIS WITH CARE. VALUABLE ADDRESSES. He then wrote to the three men whose names he had given in the letter.

He went to Hester's for dinner, for she had begged him not to leave her solitary, or even worse, with Hattie, who, knowing only part, kept adding to it all her own wild surmises.

"I can't eat," Hester said finally, as the food lay untouched on her plate. "I've never felt so shaken. Yet, to all the few who know in Sackville and Westbrook and to anyone who might hear the story, it would seem a childish matter to be smiled at, a passing trifle."

"Romeo and Juliet were just about their ages. Their love was intense enough and so is this. Anyone who had looked in that boy's eyes — "

They had lingered over their coffee and now they heard a

car in the drive. Hester hurried to the door and Melissa came in carrying a sewing bag.

"He hasn't come?" Her lips hardly formed the words. But at once there were steps on the walk and the portico. Justin opened the door. For one brief moment as the boy's eyes met those of Melissa, Hester saw the shining fire Justin had tried to describe to her.

"Come right in here," he was saying now, leading the way as Hester had asked, to the small library behind the living room. "You will be entirely undisturbed. The shades are drawn. Mrs. Carr and I will be in the dining room having another cup of coffee. Hattie has gone up to her own room. As I said, you are entirely alone."

For one hour Justin paced the dining room floor between cups of coffee. Hester sat still, her lips sometimes moving.

At exactly nine, the car returned, this time stopping in front of the house where the blast of the horn could be heard. The two in the library came out. Mac stood in the living room doorway. Melissa, after one long, white look toward him, murmured a thanks to Hester and slowly, so slowly, went out. Mac still stood, motionless.

"Sit down, my boy," Justin said. "Sit down until you can get control."

Hester and Justin sat down too, devoid of speech. The still stricken face across from them seemed beyond the power of words. Then they came from the boy himself. He leaned his elbows on his knees and put his head in his hands, while suddenly sobs shook him. He was strongly built, but he shuddered beneath them.

"Oh God!" he said, as though no one but the Deity, he felt, was in the room. "Oh God, I *can't go!* I can't leave her and never see her again. Oh God, I can't do it! It's too much for me!"

Then he raised his head, still speaking as though to an unseen presence. "But I know I'm not for the likes of her. If I had took to books an' gone on to school somewhere an' mebbe got to be a perfessor or something. But books come hard. I'll mebbe just have a trade or work in a store. It wouldn't do for the likes of her. Oh God!"

Only once more the sobs paused and then too, Mac spoke, explaining as to the Deity alone. "She wanted me to take her with me. She had money an' clothes in the sewing bag. I couldn't do that to Melissa. She's so young. She don't know." Then a last despairing cry shook him. "Oh God, *what can I do? I can't go!*"

After that there was silence until the two listeners heard the boy say, almost in a whisper, "I give my word. I guess I gotta' keep it."

It was then Justin hurried to him, for Mac's body seemed to slump in the chair. He collected himself quickly though and refused help, or food of any kind.

"I guess I was sort of talkin' to myself," he said. "You must excuse me."

In the hall, Justin put the envelope into Mac's pocket. "Addresses. May be of help. Take good care of it. Keep me in touch."

Hester put her hands on his face and kissed his forehead. He kept his head bowed for a moment as if for her blessing, then raised it and with a word of thanks, walked erectly to the door and went out into the night.

CHAPTER SIX

HESTER was wrong in one of her suppositions. There were many more than a few, both in Sackville and Westbrook, who took the short, tragic love affair of Mac and Melissa seriously enough. Of course, there were some men, who, knowing Bill Quinn's temper, did laugh it off. "I'd like to have heard his language when he ordered the kid to clear out. And I'll bet it all cost him a pretty penny, too!" But most fathers were quiet and began to talk to the boys who, shaven and suited, or long-haired and bearded like the pard, came to pick up the young girls to go where? To come home when? These fathers never got very far with their efforts to bridge the gap. The girls were embarrassed and the boys watched their elders with a deep, disconcerting wisdom in their eyes, albeit their responses were unfailingly polite.

But the mothers! Oh, the mothers! They all knew first

that Melissa was sick. At least, in a sort of gentle, undemanding prostration, she lay in bed, day after day. The doctor had been called and examined her carefully.

"Sound as a dollar, my dear," he pronounced. "A few extra vitamins and lots of fresh air will cure you. You're just run down."

Melissa had looked startled at the words. "Yes, like a clock," she said, adding with a faint smile, "and maybe I'll never strike again."

The doctor felt his simile had been well received and, patting her hand, had gone his cheerful way.

But the mothers who heard of this were both anxious and tender. They had once been young and remembered sometimes an ember from long-past fire. The story Hester told them of Mac's starting out into the night after the brief farewell touched them. So, most of the mothers were anxious, but not angry. They made better headway with the young men, bearded or shaven, than their husbands did. They began earnestly to read the sports sections of the paper. They saw the couples off from the front door, many of them, in their deep concern, quite unconsciously laying a hand on the boy's shoulder saying, "You'll drive carefully, Tom," or Dick or Harry as the case might be.

The boy always grinned and said, "Of course, I certainly will," while the girl said, "Oh, *Mother!*"

It could not be said that the new romance caused the first anxiety the parents of Westbrook had experienced for their sons and daughters. There had been many grave conferences on drugs, alcoholism and sex behavior in the evening P.T.A. meetings. But this was different. It was, in a peculiar way, personal.

In Sackville, the news spread in a few hours. Bony, to whom Mac had always been an idol, was wildly and profanely inconsolable. His gang joined him in vituperation if not in grief. The men were angered.

"So one of our kids ain't good enough to walk with one of *their* kids. Mac should of stayed an' shamed them out!"

"That's what I say!"

"You'll see, when some of those Westbrook bastards come honeyin' round, asking if I'd come up quick an' put the screens in? Who's goin' to make them wait a damned long time?" Bill Hoover smote his breast. "Me!" he said, and then louder, "Me, I'm tellin' you."

The men did little work the next day or two. They talked with bitterness. Something they had not been aware of had been hurt to the quick. This was pride, the deep instinctive pride of a man who feels himself as a human being, useful, assured and untouchable within his limitations. They all knew they couldn't be a banker like Quinn; neither could he shingle a roof or even drive a nail straight, for some of them had seen him try. So what made him and all them other hoity-toities so big that he dared to send one of *their* boys off to nowhere. No sir, Mac was good enough for anybody and they'd say so quick and proper when they got the chance.

The women were quieter. They didn't join the men's talk. In small groups and often in twos, they spoke of where Mac might be by then and whether he would ever write. They spoke of Melissa, still not well, so the report ran, but sort of weak and pale and going to a boarding school, it was said, after the holidays. They were not angry, even Mac's mother. They had experienced what the men had not.

Most of them knew what it was like to iron damask tablecloths like satin and napkins edged with delicate lace in Westbrook houses. They had shined great silver candelabra and polished crystal glasses, upon all of which the tall tapers would send their soft pools of light, as guests sat at dinner. The women knew all this and much more about the way of life in Westbrook, so their hearts were not now angered. They felt only grief and a dull acceptance.

Mac's mother had gone out once and stood a long time looking up and down the slatternly Sackville street, then came in, laid her head on the kitchen table and wept. When she roused at last, she murmured, "He was right, Mac was. No matter how he'd try, he's not for the likes of Melissa. I've seen her at home an' I know."

Then she began to make a sugar bun for Bony's lunch and practice a smile to cheer his heart which was still unpacified.

As to Justin's reception in Sackville after it was all over, he himself felt nervous and practiced speech after speech to use when he would ultimately face the boys. When he walked up to the silent group, gathered together, waiting for him at the practice hour, his legs were shaking beneath him. He began, "I just want to say — " And then his careful speeches all flew to the winds. He turned his back and walked away from them. The boys stood looking at each other and at him. They could see once for a moment something white in his hand. Then they moved in a body to where he still stood. Strangely, it was Bony who broke the silence.

"Come on, Mr. Justin. We gotta' get goin'. That last

piece didn't go so good. Hurry up, you cats, shake a leg!"

The sad story of Mac and Melissa was not mentioned, then or ever, to Justin by his young musicians. He had been absolved from all complicity. And the boys repeated their findings to their elders.

In a surprisingly short time on both sides of the high hill, then, there was little said and outwardly, it would seem, little thought of what some women, to Hester's dislike, referred to as "the episode."

But beneath this smooth surface Justin himself had deep and vital problems. The children's skill was increasing far beyond his hopes and it was now the first week of December. He *had* to beard several lions and the task made him shudder with fear.

"Say, Mr. Justin, ain't we havin' an entertainment 'round Christmas time?"

"We certainly are."

"Where's it goin' to be at?"

"We're not quite sure yet. We can always have it here."

"Here?" Shouts of misery arose. "Oh, Mr. Justin! Why here, you couldn't even get a louse in after the parents come. Aw, Mr. Justin, there's got to be *some* place!"

Justin always tried to smile and look wise.

He went first of all to the principal of the Junior High School and presented his case, as he hoped, casually. The schoolman was deeply sympathetic. He had grown up on the wrong side of the tracks himself, though far enough away that Westbrook never knew it.

"I am truly sorry, Justin. But this idea of yours has somehow got around and the parents are upset. Some of your boys and girls are really high school age, aren't they?"

"Yes, if the facts were known and they had a school to go to. You'll be surprised when you hear these children — the Drum and Fife Corps — they're really *good,* and the chorus! I'm sure it's better than any in Westbrook. Now, you see — "

"It's no use, Justin. I can't do it. I'm sorry as I can be. But these people think they're the Lord's anointed or something and if we bring the Sackville kids in here they will make trouble. I think they would hurt the kids. I don't mean physically. So it's no dice."

Sick at heart, but still doggedly determined to hope, he next saw the principal of the High School. Here, they met more nearly on a level, socially and academically. Justin made his plea quietly, but with more eloquence than he realized, while Case, the principal, listened with his eyes on his desk.

"So, first of all, I can promise a really good entertainment as I've outlined it to you and, second, I believe you have a moral obligation to do this kind, this wonderful thing, which may even wipe out old bitterness. Can I count on you, Mr. Case? It's an opportunity, a challenge in concrete form, to do what the world is talking about just now. Can't I count on you, Case?"

The principal slowly shook his head. "The thing you have in mind somehow leaked out. I heard of it a week ago, but said nothing. But at Monday's board meeting it was soon clear the men had all not only heard it but were really ready to do battle against it. They were absolutely implacable. I reasoned with them. I did my best to no avail whatsoever. Only one board member spoke up for the plan. When a vote was taken, he was the only *aye.*"

"Tom Masters, I suppose," Justin said bitterly.

"Well, yes, as a matter of fact it was. How did you know?"

"Because he's a truly good man."

"You imply the others are not?"

"Not good enough."

"I'm a member ex officio," Case said with a touch of anger. "What is your opinion of me?"

"I believe you could have stood out longer against the board's vote."

"And lose my job?"

"Would it mean that?"

"In this matter it very well could, and I'm *not* giving up my position."

"I see," said Justin. "Of course you wouldn't do that. Thank you for your time, Mr. Case. And your efforts," he added as he went to the door.

As he started out, Case came after saying, "But can't you see? For a small thing like this. How could I jeopardize — ?"

But Justin was already on the stairs.

The schools, of course, had held the natural promise, Justin felt, for the auditorium. Now these hopes had failed utterly. There remained but one more which he had left to the last because it was unrelated to the general scholastic area. This was the Parish Hall of St. Paul's Episcopal Church. In size and acoustics, it would be perfect. It even already had a stage! But the fact that Sackville had little dealings with religion in general, and with its one small dilapidated church in particular, made it seem to Justin almost too presumptuous to ask such a big favor of St. Paul's. He attended service there with Hester occasionally and had had many chats with the rector, Dr. Howard, whom he liked. After all, if there was a moral obligation connected with his plan, St. Paul's *should* be the one to accept it. He pondered this as he decided to put his courage to the test at once rather than have the torture of uncertain waiting.

He had telephoned the two principals before going to see them, but he knew Dr. Howard was always in his study at this hour, so he went straight there. As he expected, the secretary told him the Doctor was in his office then and she knew would be glad to see him. She announced the caller and withdrew.

Dr. Howard came from behind his desk with a warm greeting.

"Why, Mr. Justin, this is indeed a pleasant surprise. Do sit down and tell me what brought you to me today. Whatever it is, I'm glad to see you."

He cleared his throat a little too loudly and, in spite of his cordial greeting, looked worried. The wrinkles, or the worry lines, all suddenly showed in his long, thin face. Justin realized how much older he looked in an ordinary suit than in his clericals.

"I'm not sure just how to approach my errand, but the simplest way is usually the best." Justin told then of his desire to help the boys and girls of Sackville. If it hadn't been for an arbitrary township line, they might even have fallen within his parish. He told of the boys with their drums and fifes and their cadet suits, of the girls in their new chorus robes. He told of their eagerness, a new anticipation in their barren lives; of their utter disappointment if no sort of auditorium was provided.

"The schools have refused. You are our last hope, Dr. Howard. What do you say?"

The rector's haggard face was full of pain. Every line had deepened. "Mr. Justin," he said, "I know all this. As you've probably heard, the plan leaked out ten days ago. People have been quietly, or *not* so quietly, talking it over ever since. I'm in the worst spot of all. With all my heart I want to lend you our Parish Hall, but every member of my church and the vestry are bitterly against it. You see, they're still worried and scared about that affair of the Quinn girl and the Sackville boy. If the Sackville children come here, don't you see, our young people will certainly come out of curiosity. They will all mingle after the program — "

"No," Justin said. "I had planned for them to leave at once after they had finished."

"Not cookies and hot fruit punch or coffee and doughnuts, which our ladies would have to provide? You couldn't send those young performers back on a cold winter night without a suggestion of hospitality. That would be worse than not having them at all."

"You're using that as a crutch," Justin said angrily. "I don't think they would ever think of such a thing — though," he added wistfully, "it would be a bit of paradise for them, it's true."

"Maybe I did just drag the refreshment part in. If it were

for another cause, the women would think nothing of the trouble. But here is the crux. This is what keeps me awake nights. I *ought* to be brave enough to override everyone's decision. The vestrymen were unanimous in their vote against it. But I'm over sixty, I've been rector here for twenty years, I love every stone in the church, I love every family. I've christened them, confirmed them, married them, buried their dead. I think, without vanity, I can say they love me. In all the years there has been peace and harmony in this church. If I do this thing, even while it may have for us a moral responsibility, I will bring bitterness, dissension and general discord and maybe an end to my own usefulness. Therefore, Mr. Justin, I can't do it and my heart aches over it. So does my conscience."

Justin rose and held out his hand. "You've been honest and most sympathetic. You are in a hard spot, much harder than the school principals. I do thank you for your understanding. Good-bye."

As he turned, Dr. Howard followed him to the door. "There is one thing I *can* do for you, I can pray. Day and night I will plead with the Lord that some way will still open up for you. Do you believe in prayer, Mr. Justin?"

"As a last resort," Justin said with a wry smile.

"No, no," said the rector. "Never *last.* Make it first and all the time between and it can work miracles."

"Thank you," Justin said wishing he had the courage to ask him to try it on his congregation, but he was in no mood for pleasantry. He felt sick and sad for the children's sake first of all and then for himself, that the great hope in his own heart might find soon the perfect time of fulfillment.

He went to Hester's and as always, with her, found balm for his spirit. She was angry, anguished and then, as usual, took the initiative, when she heard his report. "I wonder," she began, meditatively, "if the seats in the Big Room could be unscrewed and set around the walls? Oh, I'll tell you, why couldn't there be two programs, one for the Little Room and one later for the adults?"

Justin took her hand and held it against his cheek. "I would never have thought of that, and we'll hang on to the ideas — "

"Unless something else turns up."

"I'm afraid that's not likely, but bless you for suggesting even a ray of hope."

"You're bitter, John?"

"I'm afraid I am. Such a small thing for Westbrook to do to bring such great happiness to the Sackville youngsters and their parents besides. Well, who am I to berate people for selfishness? The worst part is to break the news to the kids, if they don't know it already. The way word gets around here defies all analysis. I'd better go on, though, and get it over."

"Not without some lunch. I would swear you haven't eaten anything all morning."

"I cannot tell a lie, ma'am."

"Come on. Let's have a little early snack and talk of other things entirely to brighten our spirits."

But Justin's mind refused to revert to common things.

"I've been waiting to tell you something. It's a dream I've had for the climax of our program if it had come off as we hoped. Do you know Liz?"

"Liz?" She repeated. "*Liz.* Well I've seen her when she's been helping out here and there and I've spoken to her. What made you ask that question?"

"Because she has one of the most magnificent voices I've ever heard. I've never seen her. She's shy as a fawn when I go to call on Snecky and ducks out the back door or into another room. But I've heard her singing in the kitchen once or twice and once I stopped the car before the house to listen. If she had had training — I declare I think she might have made Opera!"

"Oh, John, you *are* carried away! Do you think she's pretty too?" — faintly sarcastic.

"I've never laid eyes on her. I've just told you she deliberately keeps out of my way."

"Guarding your virtue."

"Hardly. But here was my dream. If we'd gotten an auditorium I wanted her hidden behind the curtain to close the program by singing "O Holy Night." Please don't breathe this. If I didn't know I could trust you completely, I would never have spoken. The idea is hopeless now, anyway, but it could have gone through and would have made a sensation and *you* would have had a major part in it all. Now just brood on that when you want a mystery!"

"John, *please* don't take this all so seriously. Your eyes look wild. You need more food and certainly more coffee. I'm worried about you."

"Nonsense! I will have another cup though and thanks so much for the lunch. I guess I did need to be fortified a little. But I'm fine now. The boys will be in school but I think I'll make a call on Snecky. He's always so pleased, poor soul, and strange bits of practical wisdom come out of him. I'm getting fond of him so it's not just a duty as it was at first."

When he was leaving Hester said roguishly, "Look carefully, you may see Liz."

But John did not follow up her jest. Instead he said, "Stand just the way you are for a bit longer so I can look at you." And he smiled.

But as he made his way to Sackville he was not smiling. He was terribly disappointed and bitter for, even though prepared for opposition, he had somehow thought Tom Masters could influence enough on the school board to swing the decision. It had not been so. Only Dr. Howard, in pain, had spoken honestly of their responsibility and his justifiable fears. Justin came to the schoolyard and it was empty except for a lean, long figure, back against a corner of the building, which he did not see until almost upon it. It was Bony.

"So they wouldn't any of them give us an auditorium," he gritted through set teeth.

Justin could only shake his head. "But how did you know?"

"I knowed," said Bony cryptically. "An' all I can say to them people that said we couldn't have one of their auditoriums, they're all of them stinkin', lousy, dirty, goddamned bastards."

"Don't swear, Bony," though somehow the boy's language was a relief to his own spirit. "But who told you?"

"Nobody. I was watchin' here an' I seen your face. I guess the other kids will get it all right just lookin' at me. I gotta' go in now. Will you be rehearsin' us like usual after school, or what?"

"Just as usual and, Bony, don't give up. We'll work something out."

"Ain't nothin' more to work out except this stinkin' school." And Bony turned mournfully around the corner.

"He took the very words out of my mouth," Justin muttered bitterly.

When he reached Snecky's house he heard Liz singing again, this time in a rising crescendo, as though she was trying to see how high the tones would reach. When she stopped Justin drew a quaking breath. "I could be wrong," he thought, "but as I'm a living man, I think she hit high C. *What* a range!"

As he hurried to knock, Snecky came on his crutches to open the door and there was no other sound in the house. Snecky, who Justin could see was very nervous and shaky, came to the point at once. "Well, sit you down an' tell me how you made out. Which of 'em took you?"

Justin shook his head.

"None of 'em?"

"None."

"Not even the *church?*"

"No, but Snecky, Dr. Howard was in distress over the thing. He said if he let the children here use their Parish Hall it would split his congregation and they've never had any dissension in all the twenty years of his rectorship. My request, you see, coming so soon after the trouble with Mac and Melissa has made all the mothers anxious and all the men more stiff-necked than ever. Can you see that, Mr. Webb?"

"Call me Snecky. I can think better then. For I'm so rippin' red-hot mad clean through, my old bean just might get workin'." He leaned back in his chair and at long intervals brought forth such utterances as "So, we ain't even fitten to put our asses on their God-holy chairs; if I had me good legs back, I'd like to kick every blasted one of them stinkers into kingdom come an' back," and last, with a quaver, "It's the kids, they built on this so an' they thought you could do anything — it's the kids — "

All at once Snecky sat up. In his usually misty eyes there was something like light. He turned them full on Justin.

"Boys doin' pretty good now on the drums?"

"It's really amazing."

"Mind where you bought them drums?"

"I certainly do. At that big old hardware store out the road from the Village Row. Now there's a place out of another century if ever — Snecky, what are you driving at?"

"Pretty big floor space there, ain't there? That is, if all the stuff they've got there was cleared out. Might be almost as big as one of them auditoriums you've been after."

Justin couldn't speak. His throat was too full.

"Now," the old man went on, "way it just hit me was if you set that drummer gang to work, they could clear that place out. There's a big back porch which was the main store long ago and it would hold a lot and there's the big shed at the side of the store an' come to that, some of the stuff wouldn't take no hurt outside if it was covered."

"Snecky! Don't go so fast. I'm so excited I'm taking this all for granted and we don't dare do that. Mr. Bostwick may not even consider letting us use his place."

Snecky grinned. "You get along out to see him an' tell

him Snecky sent you. Him an' me was old checker buddies. I was the only one could beat him. You go an' I'll bet you'll have all the deetails settled when you come back. Funny how this thing just struck me, Mr. Justin, unless — " he drew a soiled slip of paper from his pocket. "You mind last time you was here, you give me this when I was moanin' about how my life had been wrecked." He handed it to Justin who took the slip.

"Read it to me again."

Justin read, *We shall not miss our Providential way.*

"I keep thinkin' there just might be some kind of a plan. Well, get on now, for God's sake, an' don't keep me sittin' here on pins an' needles longer than you have to."

"Snecky, I can't thank you." Justin's voice was unsteady.

"Who wants thanks? *Scat!*"

Justin had walked the distance from Westbrook thinking the exercise might help to calm his sad and bitter heart. Now, although weak from the various stresses and strains of the morning, he still took the hill and the rough dirt road at a good pace and found himself at last on the smooth highway. Here he hurried along, checking street after street until he reached Hester's own. Then he turned and all but ran until he stood at her door, breathing hard. At the sound of the knocker there came a soft bark from Flushie and then, suddenly, Hester herself, eyes wide!

"John! Something's happened. Who relented? You look like a different man from the one at lunchtime. *Tell me!*"

"No one's relented, but Snecky, of all people, had an idea. You know where we bought the drums?"

"At Bostwick's Hardware store! But what — ?"

"Well, get a coat and come along to the car. Snecky says he thinks there might be possibilities in it. It seems he's an old crony of Bostwick's, and we're to get there fast and talk to him. Snecky made it all sound so reasonable that first I lost my head too. But after all, we can't miss any sort of chance, that's sure."

As he spoke, Hester was silent, looking off into the distance. Justin watched her with interest, for he knew this was a sign she was thinking deeply. At last she spoke, still as though in a dream. "If all the stuff could be moved out there's tremendous floor space — the long counter could be just covered with greens and holly — "

"Hester, don't, please. You mustn't build on this nebulous idea and then be disappointed."

"This isn't nebulous," she said. "It's practical and I think it's going to work."

It took three rings at the bell before Bostwick himself emerged from the back office, looking disgruntled.

"I'd just thought of the goldarndest move that would sew him up tight when that there bell rung. Well," he ended mournfully, "can't be helped."

"Go on back and finish your game, Mr. Bostwick. Mrs. Carr and I are in no hurry. When you're through we want to have a little talk with you and get some advice."

"Advice from *me!* Well, I'm a billy goat's uncle! Last time anybody asked me for advice was 'bout ten years ago when a woman wanted to know how to make sassafras tea. Well, I'll hurry along. I think I've got him if he didn't move a piece when I was gone. Coupl'a chairs there. Make yourselves comfortable."

Justin and Hester began at once to take stock of the place. There was no doubt that the floor space would be enormous if the vast miscellany of stock, ranging from great canisters of unground coffee, boxes of nails, cans of maple syrup, rolls of twine, a huge jar of hoarhound drops, a fine assortment of iron skillets and modern pans, on the long counter, to the frightening and heavy complexity occupying half the space on the other side, was removed. Here was an old sleigh, its heels in the air, a superannuated spring wagon; lawn mowers, cultivators, corn planters, a couple of old Singer sewing machines, a corner cupboard filled with dishes, a coal range —

"And that's not half." Hester laughed, as Justin kept enumerating.

"It really looks hopeless," he said. "I don't think the boys could clear all this out even if Bostwick gave them leave to try. I'd pitch in of course, but my muscles aren't as strong as theirs and I wouldn't want to ask any of our Westbrook friends to help."

"What about the Sackville men?"

"More enthusiasm than work, I fear."

"Now don't think one pessimistic thought. This is going to be done. Oh, here he comes," as Bostwick came out of the office rubbing his hands in glee. "I beat him," he said. "Yes sir, beat him with that move I was tellin' you about. If you'd ever like a game, Mr. Justin, come 'round some evening. Well, now, what's on your minds? Whatever 'tis, I'm glad to see you."

Justin hesitated a second and then, beginning with the purchase of the drums, he told the whole story. Bostwick, whose expression sometimes seemed like that of a child of ten, sat now, his wise old eyes riveted upon Justin, his face set in a stern intensity as though he feared to miss a word. When the narrative reached the point of the refusal of the auditoriums, Bostwick suddenly yelled, "The church too?"

Justin nodded. "And as I was telling all this to Snecky, he said to come to you and you might have some idea."

"And you're darned right I have one," the old man hissed. "I'm goin' to get the best of them highfalutin Westbrook buggers if it's the last thing I do. What's wrong with this place if we clear it all out? We've got foldin' chairs too, enough to seat the town, stacked away somewhere. People seem to think the undertakers' is fancier now so they haven't been usin' ours so much, but we got 'em all right. An' mebbe you don't know, but I *like* them Sackville kids. They come up here sometimes an' sit around an' chew the fat with me. I think they'd clean this out like nobody's business. What say, Mr. Justin?"

"I'm past speech," Justin said, "because I'm so amazed and happy. We came to plead or even argue with you if we had to and here you've thrown your whole place right into our lap. How can we thank you?"

"Rats! I'm gonna' have the time of my life! I'll get my hired man stirred up too. He don't do nothin' he can help, but I'll betcha' he'll get het up over this. Send your Sackville boys out after school an' they can start movin' the stuff that's in here. The big farm machinery we keep in the shed that joins this buildin'. You've noticed it. But there are wide slidin' doors between and them Sackville kids are tough as nails, they can shift this stuff over. Then when the floor's all open an' cleared, you can plan how you want to do things. By jumpin' jiminy, I think we're goin' to have fun an' rub them Westbrook noses in the mud while we're doin' it. Go ahead now. Tell me what all you're goin' to do in your show."

As Justin and Hester together, prompting each other, gave the program as they hoped it would be, Bostwick grew more and more excited, adding suggestions. "You can set the chairs in aisles like, mebbe — an' a platform! Say, we always keep some lumber. One of them Sackville men would knock it up for your program — that long rack can just be moved right out to the back porch. Well, well, if I ever live to hear them young drummers and fifers — you say they got special suits an' all?"

Hester went over to the old man suddenly and kissed his cheek. He started as if he had been shot. "By jumpin' jiminy, Miss Hester, here I've had 'bout all the excitement I can stand an' you go an' put the cap sheaf on it. I'm a billy goat's uncle if what you done ain't about the nicest thing ever happened to me. I won't wash that cheek for a week, I'm tellin' you!"

"But you must treat them both alike," she said gaily and kissed the other one.

He put his bony arms around her and for a minute held her close. "You'd never believe it, but long ago I had a sweetie with hair the color of yours. Anyhow, I haven't been as happy since Hector was a pup." He looked slyly past to where Justin was standing. "There's a younger fellah around. Don't forget him."

"Oh, I won't," Hester said and then hastily went back to the description of the entertainment.

When they left at last, they had accomplished an amazing amount of practical planning. Bostwick said the boys could come out any time and start their work, for the sooner the place was cleared the sooner practice there could begin. As they tried to thank their benefactor, they found the gratitude all going the other way.

"I'll never tell you how pleased I am over this here shebang comin' in my own place. Tell Snecky I can't thank him enough for thinkin' of it. Have some posters made," he called as the car started. "Put 'Bostwick's Hardware Theayter' on, an' everybody'll know where it is."

They couldn't talk fast enough on the way back. Justin stopped the car at Hester's and was preparing to help her out when she smiled up at him roguishly and said, "Shall I follow Mr. Bostwick's advice about the way to treat younger men also?"

She felt his withdrawal. "Please don't," he said. "If you did I wouldn't be responsible for the consequences. You've been so patient. The women must have teased you just as the men have twitted me about our friendship. Can you wait a little longer? Just until this show is over and then I will have a strange story to tell you and a question that's life or death to me, to ask you. Will you wait?"

"Of course," she said, smiling, "on one condition. That you won't forget to ask the question!"

His strained face suddenly relaxed in a broad grin. "You're a little hussy, but I can assure you I won't forget the question. Now to spread the great news to Snecky and the kids. Don't forget to tell Hattie," he called as the car started.

Once on the rutty street of Sackville, Justin parked his

car and, with a *whoop* now and then, made his way to Snecky's. School had just been dismissed and in a moment he had a crowd around him, yelling questions.

" 'Loyshus, open the door and tell your grandfather we're all out here," he told the boy. And in a moment Snecky, in his wheelchair, sat in the doorway with Justin on the step before him.

"It's good news, boys and girls, and it's all due to Mr. Webb here. Now keep quiet and I'll tell you all about it."

When he had finished pandemonium reigned. Justin let them alone as they yelled, pummeled each other, shouted hurrahs for Snecky, for Justin himself and for Brown too, who, hearing the clamor, had emerged from the schoolhouse. At last there was a call for quiet.

"I've told you the good news, now I'll tell you the hard part."

"I knowed there was a catch to this," 'Loyshus growled.

"The only catch," Justin said quickly, "is that in order to have our show there's a lot of work will have to be done."

Bony spat ostentatiously upon his hands and rubbed them together. "Lead me to it," he yelled. "Whatja' say, you cats?"

The response was unanimous. The only question being when they could start. A fringe of men stood behind the boys and the women stood in their doorways, listening eagerly.

"Some of us fellahs could mebbe lend a hand," one man said above the confusion.

"We'll need a stage built later when the place is cleared." Justin said.

At once, there was a chorus of recommendation. "Bill

Hoover there is the best carpenter 'round. Bill could do it, couldn't you, Bill?"

"We'd certainly be pleased if you could," Justin added.

Bill's face had something on it resembling a sneer. "Well now, *Mr. Justin,* I don't believe I'd hardly have the time, but you can easy get another man."

"Oh certainly," Justin returned coolly. "No trouble at all. And, Mr. Brown, I was wondering if the boys could make a beginning right now and work for an hour or so following the afternoon session each day. When they get a clear floor we'll invite the chorus in to have a look and plan the decorations and so forth. Could this be arranged?"

"Surest thing you know. I'll come along now and lend a hand. There's heavy stuff there."

"And I'll be there of course and Bostwick's hired man. *Let's go!*" he shouted.

Bony and his group started off on foot over the hill. "We know a shortcut," he called back. The others were packed into Justin's and Brown's cars. They all met at the store where Bostwick wore what could be called a seraphic grin. And the work began.

As Justin lay in bed many nights sleepless from excitement, he thought of Dr. Howard's troubled conscience, of his strained face as he refused the request and then of the sudden shining light in his eyes as he offered the gift of his prayers and, from them, the possibility of a miracle. Could there be such a thing? Justin wondered. Could there have been some nebulous supernatural thread that ran from the first purchase of the drums from Bostwick, all through practice on and off, the refusal of the auditoriums which led to Snecky's righteous anger which, in turn, led full circle back to Bostwick and the hardware store. "Strange," he kept thinking. But he certainly didn't believe in miracles. Of this he was sure. And yet —

But while the floor of the store had been cleared as though elves had been working in the night, and the stage and a platform below, with steps leading to the aisles, had been built with much measuring and pounding, the boys, out of the corners of their mouths, asked many questions.

"What's eatin' Bill Hoover that he wouldn't make the stage?"

"He just sort of sneered at Mr. Justin."

"An' he hasn't done a damned piece of work for three weeks, the stinker."

"You know," Bony whispered, "I could be wrong, but it just strikes me he's got it in for Mr. Justin."

"What for?"

"How would I know? Just something stickin' in his craw, I s'pose."

There was tremendously important work of a different sort going on every day. It began on an afternoon when Hester knocked on the door of Snecky Webb's house and, at his feeble answer, bounced quietly in.

"It's Liz I really want to see. Oh Liz, wait a minute. I'd like you to do something for me. And oh, could I have a cup of tea?"

Liz turned slowly from the back door. She had worked once or twice for Mrs. Carr — just ironing napkins and such, so she didn't have to be shy.

"Hello, Mrs. Carr. How's the show comin' on? I'll make some tea right away."

"If I told you, Liz, you wouldn't believe me about the

show. It is simply fantastic how those children have taken hold of it, now that they have a real place to practice. And some of the Westbrook people have quietly helped behind everybody's back, I guess they are ashamed now. Mrs. Masters has been on our side from the first and now she's dug up a really stunning curtain that the women's club had discarded and the men have hung it on wires across the stage so it can be pulled back and forth. Oh, how thrilled the youngsters are over that curtain!"

Hester set down her teacup and leaned across the table. "And now, Liz, I come to my real favor. We are arranging the program: Drum and Fife Corps ushering in the chorus and then each group performing for some time alone. Then there will be Christmas carols with the whole audience joining. All this time the curtain will be drawn. Then suddenly it will be pulled back and there will be the manger scene. I think about twenty women have contributed to that. It's *beautiful.* You know your 'Loyshus is to be Joseph, don't you? He will speak plainly and he will sing the solo part beautifully."

"I'm awful proud of 'Loyshus," Liz said.

"Then," Hester went on, "as soon as the manger scene is over the curtain will be drawn again and from behind it where no one can see the singer, I want someone to sing the greatest Christmas song of all — "O Holy Night." After that, Dr. Howard will pronounce the benediction and all will be over. But Liz, the beauty of it! We've never had a Christmas entertainment like this!"

"It sounds nice," Liz said very slowly. "I'd like to hear it. Who's to sing the song at the end?"

"*You* are, Liz."

She drew back as though she had been struck. "Me?" she said. And again, "Me?"

"None but you. You have the greatest voice in all these towns. You can make us feel it! You can lift us as on angels' wings, because you have suffered, Liz."

"You know why I couldn't, Mrs. Carr."

"You'll be behind the curtain. No one will see you or even recognize your voice. No one will have heard it as you will sing then. Don't you see?"

"But *me,*" Liz kept saying with tears on her cheeks. *"Me!"*

"None but you! It will be the disappointment of the whole occasion if you refuse. Think of the pride of 'Loyshus and Vi'let when they know afterward!"

"But other folks could see me afterward too!"

"No, that will be arranged. I'll take and bring you in my car and we'll go through Mr. Bostwick's kitchen. You'll do it, Liz, if I teach you the music? You'll love singing it."

"I've always wanted to let my voice out but I was afraid to, here."

As Hester was leaving, Liz threw her arms around her neck. "Oh, thank you for wanting *me,*" she said. "And I'll try hard to learn the song."

The rest was easily arranged. It was no surprise to Westbrook ladies that Hester was doing over all her small linens and having Liz iron them. She came each morning and the practice took place in the small library where Mac and Melissa had said their good-bye.

"There's a small piano here that was mine when I was a girl and I never could bear to part with it. Here you can let your voice out as much as you please, as you couldn't in the drawing room. Now first let me play the music and try the words quietly though I'm no singer. Then you can learn both. Here's a copy for you."

Hester played the song softly, then louder, singing the words as she did. Then Liz sang with her. It was plain she had a keen ear for music. In a few repeats she had caught the melody and the beauty of the words. Day after day, there, the great voice rose and fell with Hester's quiet training adding to its smoothness and depth. Hester refused absolutely to give any report of the practice, though Justin teased her about her secretiveness. She only smiled as though she herself had seen a miracle and said she wanted to surprise him. "And no one, even you, is to set foot behind that curtain, for unless the lady there is kept a mystery she does not sing. You haven't dropped a hint to any of the men?"

"Hardly."

"I've had some questions from the girls when she was reaching a glorious note as they passed by and an echo reached them but I told them we were training a strange soloist as a surprise. Someone I knew. They are terribly excited. They say *everybody's* coming! Oh, John, if nothing goes wrong! I'm driving over in my car with Liz and bringing her back."

"Why, I had expected to do that. I've got to take Snecky anyway. His being at the show will be a sort of *nunc dimittus* for him, you know. But I'd like to bring Liz and let them both have a sort of little reception when she comes out from behind the curtain."

"I'm so sorry, John, but she's adamant and she *won't* come out. I'm afraid if she goes — and I really think now she will — it will have to be shrouded in my car and home the same way. I'm terribly disappointed too. I wish I could change things."

"Never mind! The great thing is to get her there. I'm having three buses for the Sackville folks. One for the performers and the others for the guests. Do you think that's enough?"

"You're not bleeding yourself financially white over all this, are you?" Her voice was anxious.

He hesitated, embarrassed. "It's not very good form to discuss money, but I must explain what is troubling you. My foster father was a very wealthy man, and as his adopted son I was his heir. So, I have plenty for my needs, thanks to him, and don't worry."

Hester stared at him in surprise. "I thought college professors sometimes had not too much for extras, but I'm thrilled that you have. The buses will be the ultimate elegance for Sackville. And how the days are flying past toward the big one!"

It was true as time itself. There came suddenly, as though neither prepared for nor expected, the week of Christmas. It was in the air with its first light, crisp snowfall; it was in the gay wreaths on the finely carved doors of Westbrook; it was in the rare attitude of jollity and excitement in Sackville never before known; it was even in the red ribbon bow in Flushie's collar which flashed after his mistress wherever she went. But even though she wore a red gown her heart was not as gay as the holly on the door.

Hattie, pausing during breakfast, spoke her mind. "An' it's not mine to say, but it does seem to me if that man's ever goin' to *speak,* it ought to be now. So you could announce it at Christmas. The two of you can't look at each other without love just showin' right out of your eyes. I tell you I think people have begun to *talk.* What's wrong with the man? Unless you're engaged and have kep' it from me."

"No, Hattie."

"Well, where would you find a nicer man and one that would take to Flushie the way he does? Some men can't abide dogs — as you very well know. Well, I've said my say. Among you be it!"

A thorn in the wound, Hester thought as she lay sleepless. She was mystified, she was crushed in spirit. For never had she known real love, until now: tender, passionate, longing. He had said again that after the show he would tell her all his story and ask her the question that meant life or death to him. And oh, as he must know, to her. But why the delay? She knew nothing of his past life except the recent disclosure of wealth. She loved him; she trusted him; but she could not bear this strange waiting much longer. What had the show to do with his intimate life that they must be linked together in her relations with him?

Even Ginny Masters said she would never have believed the hardward store could look as it did. A theater decked with Christmas and sweetly redolent with balsam and spruce! Tom, still annoyed at his stiff-necked fellow board members, had taken over with Justin the making of the posters, so all along the Row, through Westbrook and Sackville, the big red cards, lettered in green, proclaimed the event, giving details of the program. For the first time, Sackville could be said to be on the map.

As Justin planned with Snecky about his getting to the show, the old man, under his excitement, was serious.

"You know that little paper you give me, Mr. Justin? I can say it, I've read it so often. *We shall not miss our Providential way.* You believe mebbe our lives are planned out — like?"

"I'm not sure, Snecky. The older I grow, the more I think it might possibly be."

"You said that before. Well, I'll just betcha' that's the way it is. I'll betcha' an' it sure relieves my mind."

Came the day, clear, frosty, with a very light snow on the ground. Came the usual minor mishaps: a choir robe ripped; a cadet suit lost entirely for an hour; one drumstick hidden for a joke, with a fight following. As to the manger scene upon which Hester and Ginny had lavished their tenderest skill, one shepherd defected entirely from pre-stage fright, but, lured by Justin's ingenious wiles, agreed to come back; one wise man dropped the casket he was taking backstage and it had to be mended entirely with Scotch tape and faith; the curtain stuck but was repaired; in fact, all the small nerve-racking things happened which usually take place before a children's entertainment. But, incredible as it seemed to all, the great buses rolled up on time, one taking on its cargo of youthful performers, supervised with every adjunct properly checked by Brown; two filled up with Sackville citizens in their brave best. Justin managed to get Snecky into his car with a folding chair in the back for his use later; Hester drove slowly with a slender figure in black coat and scarf beside her; and at "Bostwick's Hardware Theayter," the crowds began filling the place.

"They'll be standing 'round the wall pretty soon," Justin whispered to Hester as they stood out of sight, surveying the scene. "How does she seem?"

"Very composed. She says at last she can sing as she's longed to do. She's waiting in Mr. Bostwick's kitchen."

Justin's eyes were shining. "When all is over, may I have a little of your time for very special business?"

"Oh John, you know — " She gave a little gulp to keep back the tears. "I left Hattie lamenting that she couldn't bring Flushie. She says he'd enjoy it. She's put an extra blanket in his little house on the porch and double-locked his chain for fear he will try to break out and follow us. She says — oh, it's almost time!"

She went to the piano at the side of the low platform below the stage and began to play softly. Justin, at the bus, lined up his carefully trained cadets and chorus. The crowd which packed the place had quieted as the music grew stronger. Then entered the girls of the chorus in their soft purple and white robes, moving up one aisle, singing "Joy to the World!" with the Drum and Fifers marching up the other one, beating a soft tattoo and fife accompaniment. The audience could not be restrained. The sight, the sound, the beauty of the robes, the incredible smartness of the cadet suits, never seen before, were all too much for them. They clapped, they cheered, they all but shouted their pleasure.

When the young performers had reached the front and lined up on the platform below the stage, Justin stepped to their side and asked for order. "I know the Drum and Fife

Corps and the Girls' Chorus of Sackville are very happy over your welcome. We will go on now with the program and I hope you will all be quiet so you can hear it. First are some tunes by the Drum and Fife Corps."

The boys took the center looking, now in full view, smarter than ever, and at a signal from Justin began their songs. They were very simple, but with a bit of rollicking in them. The recorders and fifettes rose shrill and clear and the drums seemed almost to carry the tunes with them. The audience was entranced. It was really, as Justin knew better than anyone else, a tour de force. The boys finally retired to the front rows of seats reserved for them, flushed and happy at their reception and proud of the little bows Justin had taught them to make.

"We will leave Christmas for a time while the Girls' Chorus sings a group of secular songs." He gave the signal and the girls stood before the audience while small sounds of approval swept over it. It was a pretty sight. Justin once met the eyes of the High School principal who dropped his own at once.

In a sense, the chorus was as much of a surprise as the cadets. The hours of patient training and practice showed now with a startling perfection for such young voices. Sure and true rose the sopranos; rich and deep the balanced blend of the altos. The songs were familiar and the audience listened breathlessly. Justin finally stepped forward.

"During the weeks of rehearsal there was one song which was a special favorite with the girls. They have asked to sing it and will do so now."

Hester gave a chord and then the voices, unaccompanied, began the "Londonderry Air." A little sound like a soft *oh* swept over the crowd. Then utter quiet as the song rose slowly again and again to its heights and sank at last into its poignant ending — *even unto death.*

A moment's hush and then tumultuous applause, as much as for the cadets, or more. The decision against encores had been made before, so now, the girls, radiant, made their bows of thanks and sat down, flushed with success.

"You may like now," Justin announced, "to change your position, so I will ask you all to stand and join together in some Christmas carols while the next scene is being made ready. I want to speak of it. It will be a short play, 'The Manger,' and when it is over, will you please refrain from applause. For just following it, as our closing number, there will be sung 'O Holy Night' as a solo. After which, Dr. Howard will pronounce the benediction. So until then, please listen quietly. But after that" — he smiled — "the lid is off. You are free to circulate about and have a good time." Out of the tail of his eye he could see Dr. Howard, tears on his cheeks, his lips moving.

The audience rose with alacrity and the old carols rang out. One after another was called for and Hester played them all. At last Justin stood before them again, to ask for quiet.

"And now, 'The Manger.' "

A Sackville man who tinkered with wiring had taken care of the electrical work, so now the curtain rose on a softly lighted scene. A painter had made the backdrop of dark blue sky and many little stars with the great one above the little stable which the older boys had built. The young Madonna in her blue robe leaned over the side of the manger; 'Loyshus stood near, with a look of wonder. "What Child is this?" he sang clearly and sweetly.

Justin had written the play using much of the traditional wording with interposed lines to make the scene more real to those who played it and those who watched. The shepherds drew near with an old song Hester had found in her scrapbook. The young Mary, as though the child were affrighted, leaned nearer, her arms unconsciously clasping the crib as she sang to many choked throats:

Hush my babe, lie still and slumber;
Holy angels guard thy bed.

The little drama moved on as the wise men came to kneel and sing "We Three Kings" as they offered their gifts. And then the light grew more dim on the chorus at the side as they sang softly, "Away in a Manger." It was over. The curtain came down and the children quietly went back to their places. Justin raised his hand again though he did not need to ask for silence. "Our closing number is a solo, 'O Holy Night.' Please be very still as you listen, with no applause."

Hester struck the opening chords and then from behind the curtain came the voice, *The Voice,* the like of which the audience had not heard before. For Liz was pouring out the long years of her yearning, her shame and repression. There was now no withholding. The glorious notes of her great inheritance filled the hall and overflowed into the hearts of her listeners.

He knows our needs,
To our weaknesses no stranger

The words were slow and clear so that none could miss their meaning. And at the last, in one great, incredible lift of song, *"O night, O night divine!"*

Justin held to the support near him. He was shaken. Even he had expected nothing like this. What, oh what, must the other listeners feel?

The curtain was still down. The benediction was spoken as the audience sat as though galvanized in their seats. Then he could see people moving about and a general confusion beginning. It was his time. There was no reason why he couldn't speak to her now. He must try to tell her, to thank her —

He stepped quickly behind the curtain. He faced the woman, the singer, in the dim light.

She spoke with a sob.

"Johnny! You shouldn't have come here. I've tried — I knew you at the very first. You haven't changed but you must never let anyone know — "

"Lib," he said. "Oh Lib, is it you?"

CHAPTER SEVEN

When Hester could at last get away from the crowd that had gathered around the piano, exclaiming over the program and almost wildly demanding the name of the soloist, she slipped back of the curtain, over the empty stage and into Mr. Bostwick's kitchen. Here Liz stood, trembling, by the door.

"Let's get away fast, Mrs. Carr. I've got to go."

"But Liz! Surely now when everyone wants to meet the singer, you have a chance to show them the woman you really are — "

"Please. You don't understand. I must get out quick."

All the way back, Hester reasoned gently with her companion, telling her again that her singing had moved the audience, as so many of them averred, as nothing else ever had. Why, why would she not let her identity be known?

Liz was silent until they reached her house. "If anyone

wants to talk to me here they can come, but I couldn't go out back there amongst all the people."

They found Snecky already there, which surprised Hester. She had not had a glimpse of Justin after the solo. He had evidently left the final shepherding of the young performers to Brown. Along with his accomplished "miracle," good old Dr. Howard had insisted on his original idea of doughnuts and hot cider for the boys and girls. It was odd for Justin to leave so quickly while this was going on.

Then a warmth like summer came over her. She felt her cheeks grow hot. Of course. After some quick congratulations he would leave to reach her as soon as possible. He might be waiting for her now with his revelation, whatever that was, and *the Question!*

She drove as fast as she could over the rough Sackville street and finally along the highway until she reached the beginning of her own. Halfway down, she saw a group in the moonlight and heard the cries in front of her house. Hattie was screaming hysterically with Justin beside her, trying to calm her. Hester's heart sank as she drove on to where several other cars were parked. She jumped out before anyone could help her. "What is it?" she called. "Hattie, what's the matter?"

"It's Flushie, that's what's the matter. Oh, Miss Hester, he's been stole. I told you we should have took him to the play and not leave him alone. Oh, we may never get him back!" She sobbed.

Justin caught one of Hester's trembling hands in one of his and held Hattie's arm with the other.

"Now quiet down, Hattie. I've just got here. Tell us all just what you found when you got home."

"I went to his little house on the porch to get him. I always warm him a bit of milk before he — "

"Yes, yes. And just what did you find?"

"I'd double-locked his chain so he couldn't possible get loose an' there it was unfastened an' he was *gone!*" Her sobs began afresh.

"Keep a good heart," John told Hester. "It looks bad at the moment, but we're sure to find him. Someone took him who knew where he would be. What would you advise doing first, Tom?"

For Tom and Ginny, after seeing Hattie safely in the house and starting off, had returned, hearing her screams. The Quinns were there too and the Lairds and the Wilsons.

"I'd say, let's get in our cars and fan out over all the nearby streets. We can call him — Hester's voice will be best — and whistle, and also stop here and there at houses to find out if they've seen him or heard anything. Cheer up, Hester. He can't be far away. We'll all come back here and plan our next move if this doesn't work."

"I'll go in an' make coffee." Hattie said, with instinctive reaction.

They set out, the voices and whistles echoing from the streets as they drove slowly along. In Justin's car there was silence except for Hester's calls. It was strange, she thought, that he didn't speak and because he did not, neither did she. She trembled, though, and her heart was heavy.

When the cars all returned to their starting point with nothing to report from out of the night, the group gratefully drank the hot coffee and, then, Justin, his face strained and pale, spoke to the others.

"I've just got an idea," he said. "I may be wrong, but I shouldn't wonder if Bill Hoover took the dog."

Hattie pounced. "An' right you are, Mr. Justin. He's always been honeying around Flushie. 'Nice little pup you got here' and 'Would you care to sell him, Mrs. Carr?' Mr. Justin, I think you've just hit on the right man. He'll have taken him to his house, I'll bet!"

"Yes," Justin said slowly. "I think he probably has. We'll go and have a look anyway. Do you mind coming along? It won't be a very savory place, so we'd better not take the girls."

"I'm coming." Hester spoke decidedly. "He'll know my voice best of all."

"Oh, let's stick together," Ginny said. "We can stay in the car if it's all that bad."

"We'll need flashlights," Justin said.

"Oh, we've got aplenty," Hattie assured him. "I keep one in every room in case of burglars or the electric goin' off."

With Hester's help, they were collected and each person supplied. "I'll lead the way," Justin said with a long look at Hester. A strange look the others thought at the time, as of one who says good-bye. But that was foolish, for she was going with him.

"We'll park at the upper end of the street," he went on, "then, since there probably will still be people about after the excitement of the evening, we can take the path that runs behind the schoolhouse and that will bring us out right at Hoover's back door. Are we ready?"

The cars started, reached at last the rough street in Sackville and then parked beside the schoolhouse. They could see many lights burning and sporadic shouts and songs rising here and there. The buses had disgorged their occupants and gone their way. Now there would be many young and old eager to talk the great evening over.

But along the path where the little group, led by Justin, made their way, all seemed dim and quiet under a bulbous moon.

At last Justin stopped at the back of a ramshackle house with a sort of lean-to, built apparently above a small cave beside the fence. As he looked, Bill Hoover himself stepped out from the porch and faced him, leering.

"Well, well!" he exclaimed. "So you haven't forgot the Robber's Cave you an' me built when we was boys, eh? Have you?"

"I thought of it only a few minutes ago on account of the dog. Hand him over, Bill. You've made enough trouble already. Let's have no more talk."

"No more talk, he says. Well now, just a minute. I've got a few things to say to these fine Westbrook people who came with you." He walked closer. "Better than I ever expected, havin' them here too. All right, Mrs. Carr. Your dog's safe. You'll have him in a minute. An' now, *Mr. Justin,* what about you?"

"What *about* me?"

"Well, there's this about you. Can you hear me, all you folks? This here fellah ain't no more *Justin* than I am. His name's John Carston an' he was born here in Sackville same as I was. I could point you out the house, only it's been tore down. His pap had been savin' money for years to buy some sort of a instrument. He was awful musical, Carston was, an' this here fellah', Johnny, stole that money out of the box his pap kep' it in an' ran away an' nobody ever seen hide nor hair of him afterward till he come struttin' back here as *Mr. Justin.* Can you deny it?" he asked.

"Just the name. My legal name is Justin. My foster father adopted me."

"A likely story!" said Bill. "An' one thing more. He's a brother of Liz, the town — "

Justin had him by the throat. "Don't say any more or I'll kill you!"

Bill shook himself loose and grinned, apparently more in amusement than anger.

"So our fellah here has some ginger in him! You wouldn't think it to look at him. I'll get your pup, Mrs. Carr. I let the kids build up the cave again every year, but I knew Johnny here would mind about it, so I used it for a trap. With the pup. It worked too. So I guess I've made my point."

He crawled under the lean-to and finally brought out Flushie, shivering and giving small moaning barks, as he was returned to his mistress.

Tom Masters found his voice from the silent group who had listened. "This was monstrous, Bill, and I'll have the law on you for stealing the dog!"

"I wasn't stealin' him. I just used him as *bait* an' it worked. I was goin' to give him back. But see, I suspicioned from the first that this here fellah was the Johnny Carston that was a kid with me. Something in his face hasn't changed somehow, but I had to be sure. Now I am, an' I thought folks ought to know. So, you've got your dog, Mrs. Carr, an' you can all be goin' along. I've said my say."

"And we'll have more to say later," Tom Masters called, as the little group started back along the path. There was silence until they came to the cars, then Justin spoke.

"If you don't mind, Hester, I would like it if you would all come into her house long enough for me to present my side of the story. Is that all right? Will you come?"

"Of course." Tom spoke again for the group.

When they reached the house, Hattie was waiting inside the house to open the door. She received Flushie with tears and hysterical thanksgiving and bore him off to the kitchen to feed and pet him to her heart's content and no one stopped her. Hester ushered the others into the drawing room and, with a stricken face, sat down in her usual place on the sofa where, for once, Justin did not join her. Instead, he stood with his back to the low fire while Ginny, and Tom especially, tried to fill in the awful silence as best they could.

"We haven't had a minute until now to speak of the entertainment! Why, it was out of this world," Ginny exclaimed. "I simply don't know how you got them all trained so perfectly, even if I was a party to some of it."

"It was the most moving thing I've seen and heard for many a day," Tom chimed in. "I'd heard about the cadet suits but you girls certainly outdid yourselves on them."

"And those *lovely* choir robes," Millie Laird said.

So it went, the program, the buses, the number of Westbrook people in the audience, the red faces, presumably, of the schoolmen and vestrymen who had refused the auditoriums, but came out of curiosity, everything was touched upon except Bill Hoover's story and because of that, and in spite of the efforts at conversation, everyone looked stunned and anxious.

At last, when he could break in, Justin said quietly, "Thank you for all you've said, but now I want to talk about what has just happened. At Bill Hoover's. I don't like to speak ill of the dead, but I think I deserve to have you know all the truth. Bill's story is substantially correct. I was born in Sackville as John Carston. My mother was dead. My father was a hard and cruel man in spite of what must have been a great talent for music."

A log fell and charred. The listeners did not move.

"One night when I was twelve, he beat me unmercifully and then left the house. I felt I could not endure it any longer. My sister Lib, as we called her, had gone out. She kept out of his way as much as she could. She was four years older than I and in my boyish way I was fond of her. I knew where the money was kept, but had no knowledge of the value or denomination of the bills. I got the box, took the contents, crammed it into my pocket and left. My one idea was to get far away from him, and to me that meant the city."

He stopped, breathing hard, and then went on. "I don't know yet how I did it for it's all vague in my mind. I know I used the bills to buy rides, holding them out to coming cars to tempt people to take me in. Many did. But the last were a bad lot. They took all the rest of the money and threw me out. It was on the edge of the city then, beside a row of brownstone fronts. I couldn't go any further and fell down on the steps of one of these. It was here that Professor Justin found me and carried me in."

There was a little cry like a sob from Hester.

"He was an elderly bachelor and lonely, the head of the Science Department in the City College. He and his housekeeper saw the condition of my bruised body and called a doctor. I was very sick for quite some time and then at last I opened my eyes and saw a man's kind face looking down at me. 'You're going to be my boy, now,' he said. And so it was. There was practically no red tape to cut. I couldn't or wouldn't tell where I came from; there was, of course, no inquiry from here; after the doctor treated me, he said never to send me back to where I had been so abused. So, after a reasonable time, I became Professor Justin's legal son and we loved each other. I was avid for learning and had the best schools and colleges and some travel. Then later, when Father Justin died, I settled down to be a professor myself. In all this time, Sackville had, consciously or unconsciously, become obliterated from my mind. But one day, some months ago, I suddenly had a wave of remembrance and a feeling that I owed some sort of debt and should come back to see. So I came. The rest you know."

For a full minute, no one spoke, then Bill Quinn cleared his throat a bit too loudly. "Well, that's an amazing story, Justin!"

"Just like a movie," Kate Wilson said. "Seriously, did you ever think of writing it out as a script and trying it? It's got everything."

"It's very moving, Justin," Tom said.

"Was the man who adopted you wealthy?"

"Yes, his family always had been, but he chose to teach."

"Well there!" Kate said triumphantly. "There's your rags-to-riches theme. You start in Sackville and end up — "

"Oh, shut up, Kate! What a thing to say! You're always trying to make movies in your head." Her husband spoke sharply. "But as to Sackville, I'd like to tell you again, Justin, that the program was really beautiful. How you and Hester trained those kids — "

"And don't forget me!" Ginny put in. "I did a lot of the work too. Oh, a good many of us did our part. And now for our reward, I think we should know the secret you've been hiding. *Who was the mysterious singer?*"

There were cries from all that the name be revealed.

Justin said quietly, "It was my sister Lib, whom I've never seen since I came until tonight, behind the curtain. She's kept out of my way for fear if the truth were known it would affect my relationship with the friends I've made here."

"You don't mean *Liz?*"

The faces of the group were stunned.

"I believe that's what everyone calls her. As a boy, I knew her as Lib."

"But that voice! It's incredible! Something ought to be done about it."

"I intend to do something about it," Justin said with an edge to his tone.

"Of course. That would now, I see, be your responsibility. But there's surely magnificent material to work on there. Well, the evening has been full of surprises, and my congratulations again for the fine program. I think we ought to be going, but" — with a rather forced laugh — "I'm afraid we may miss something. Something else exciting," said Quinn.

"It's certainly been quite an evening and I'll never forget the performance those kids put on, nor the great voice at the end. Merry Christmas, Justin and Hester and everybody. We really ought to be getting along now, too," came from Millie Laird.

So the good-byes went, as couple after couple rose, got their coats and departed. Congratulations over and over on the program, repetition of details, all good wishes and a merry, merry Christmas! Justin's own story was referred to not at all!

Tom and Ginny Masters were the last to leave. Tom held out his hand and Justin grasped it. "You're our friend, old man, and we don't give a damn where you were born. I could cheerfully wring Bill Hoover's neck myself, but it mightn't be such a good idea at that. Well, good night, after a great success, and may you both have a gratified feeling over it and a very happy Christmas."

Ginny kissed Hester, her eyes full, and then laid her hand tenderly on Justin's arm, but did not speak.

When they were at the door, Tom turned. "I hate to say this, Justin, but it's the only thing that troubles me. If Bill Hoover hadn't got his dirty work in, did you intend to continue keeping your early life a secret?"

"No, no!" Justin cried. "I'm glad you asked and I should have made that clear to all the rest. You see, when I came here and first saw Sackville, I had a terrible feeling of shock.

My memory of it, as I've said, had not been clear. As I felt then, it was no time to tell all my new Westbrook friends that I had been born there. I couldn't have done it with any dignity whatever. Then I began to work with the children and the idea came to me that if they could ever achieve something beautiful in the eyes of Westbrook, my own story then would not be all sordid. So I waited. All during the program, when it went so perfectly, I kept saying to myself, 'I was wise, I was wise.' After this I can tell my story to those" — he glanced at Hester — "who are closest to me. But you see, it didn't work out that way. Maybe I was a coward."

"No," Tom said slowly. "I think I can follow your psychology entirely. Glad you told me, though. And now, good night again."

When they had gone, Hester and Justin still stood, looking at each other with stricken faces.

"Bless Tom. He was the only one who shook my hand. You saw the look on the others' faces?"

"Yes, but — "

"They are shocked and still stunned by the various revelations tonight. I am not the man they thought they were receiving into their homes, to their dinner tables. The memory of Bill Hoover's ugly report right amid his dirty surroundings will rise up unconsciously in their minds. I'm the boy from Sackville who was beaten, stole all his father's money and ran away. *That's* what they will remember first, last and always."

"But, John, that is not what *I* will remember. Can't you just think of us?"

"Oh, my dear! My dear! I have to come to that. Sit down. You're so white."

"So are you. Can't you, as I say — ?"

He still stood, one hand on the mantel as though for support. His face was haggard.

"I can't, Hester. All I had planned for tonight has been ruined. It's worse than being beaten in body. I'm bruised in heart. My spirit is broken and I am a man of pride. I will not allow myself to be condescended to, as I was tonight. I have walked in dignity now for many years. I intend to continue to do so."

Hester had sunk down on the couch exhausted; now she rose and stood looking at him with a coldness in her gray eyes.

"Can you possibly mean you are leaving me? That you are going away?"

He bowed his head. "I must," he said in a stricken voice. "I must look this all over alone and get a new perspective. Also if I'm not among them every day, it will give the Westbrook people a chance to think it all over and perhaps to change the views they hold now. Can't you see this, Hester?"

"No, I can't," she said.

He took a step nearer her and then drew back, for her voice was cold.

"And what about me?" she said.

He spoke very low. "You can forget me, or you can hate me — or you could still be patient with me, for tonight, after what I dreamed of telling you with my very soul on fire, I seem to be only an empty shell filled with ashes, if you understand."

"I don't believe I do."

"No, I see that you don't. I'm sorry. The best thing I can do now is to leave." And he moved into the hall and got his coat. Hester followed him and said nothing. At the door without a touch, or a parting caress, he said hesitantly, "If I come back, will you forgive me?"

"I don't know," she said, her voice still cold. "You could try."

He stood a long moment looking at her and then, even as Mac had done, went out like a wanderer into the night.

When the door closed, Hester sank down on the hall chair and gave way to the sobs she had been stifling with difficulty. Hattie, hearing them, emerged with Flushie who made a leap to his mistress's knee.

"An' what's the matter with you, Miss Hester, never paying any attention to your little dog here, moanin' his heart out for you? Is Mr. Justin gone? An' what's wrong now? Don't tell me he's spoke an' you *refused* him!"

There was plenty of talk on the commuter train the next morning and at the last pre-Christmas luncheons. It was the sort of dramatic conversation that women love and men do not scorn. Of course, there was the matter of the excellent entertainment to discuss, with much explanation of the refusal of the auditoriums by the schools and church and a tendency to shift the intransigence to someone else. "Now, I really wouldn't have been too much against the kids using our school, but you know how Bill Quinn is and he had a lot of followers — " and so on and so on.

But the vital subject before both men and women of Westbrook was John Justin. The entertainment was past.

This man with a new and unsavory background was, and would continue to be (so they thought) in their midst. What a story for constant repetition! What a shock to everyone! How was he to be treated now? "The same as always!" Tom Masters kept saying a little angrily. "How else?"

Well, it was argued, to say the least, it was embarrassing, especially the fact that he was the brother of *Liz.*

"What do you make of that, Tom?"

"Well, as for me," Tom said, scanning the club car group with cool eyes, "I've never made *anything* of that."

At which point, several men suddenly became interested in their newspapers.

But, for the women, there was a double subject upon which they bared their opinions. Justin's story, of course, with its every detail, but also that of Hester! What would all this new revelation do to her? For somehow, in their women's hearts, they surmised that the ugly scene at Bill Hoover's which they had either seen or had had minutely described to them, might bring a faint beclouding over the golden light of love which seemed to hover above the two. Most of them had known Hester for some years, first as the patient, young wife of the demanding Walter, then as the gentle *relict,* as she always insisted upon being called to avoid the word *widow,* during which time, she quietly refused to consider the male advances that her beauty of face and nature drew to her; and now, as of these last months, they had all seen her come alive as a new woman, laughing, glowing, her whole being seeming to glisten in the light of love called forth by John Justin, the newcomer to the town. And on his part, there had been a noticeable response, a sudden warmth of eye and smile as he looked upon Hester. Oh, they were in love, that was certain. And now, would all this which everyone was busily discussing make any difference?

Just after New Year's, the news spread that Justin had gone away. He was known to have made many calls in Sackville, then had locked his little house, given a key to Tom Masters and left town. No one knew where he had gone. If Tom knew, he was not saying, and certainly no one when they saw Hester's tired eyes asked her. So the winter went on without the joys which had made those of the last year so happy. At night Hester paced her room, too restless to sleep. Flushie, at the foot of her bed, lay crouched on his paws watching her anxiously, knowing something was strangely wrong. Hester thought of the night he had been stolen. If he had only been inside then, how different her life might now be. But the little house on the porch was used when the weather was not cold. Here, Flushie could be put to bed with a bone to gnaw and a somewhat unsavory blanket he particularly loved. As soon as real cold came on, he spent his nights with her.

Now, as she walked back and forth, her thoughts were turbulent like the weather outside. January had been mild, but February was tempestuous. So was Hester's heart. I love him. *I hate him.* I'll never forgive him. *I'll take him back on any terms whatever.* He's selfish and cruel to go off and leave me. *Oh, I can understand his shock and bitter pride.* So her thoughts contended for the mastery, until, finally, Hattie would appear at her door.

"Now stop this pacin' around. A body can't get any rest knowin' you're walkin' the floor. Look, you're even keepin' the pup awake. Get along to your bed. If Mr. Justin comes back, you can do what you please an' if he don't come, there's as good fish in the sea as ever — You know, Miss Hester, I miss him myself somethin' awful an' that's the honest truth."

There were weekly notes from him which somehow failed to bring Hester comfort. Each began, *My very dear,* and went on to say he was fighting his battles out on nightly walks, but on the campus, where no one would mistake him for a burglar. After some such meager news as this, he asked her forgiveness and signed himself, *Yours always, John.* Not much upon which to feed a hungry heart!

One week instead of a letter there were only a few lines from a poem. Hester read them over and over.

> A flower has opened in my heart . . .
> What flower is this, what flower of spring,
> What simple, secret thing?
> O flower within me, wondrous white,
> I know you only as my need
> And my unsealèd sight.

During the first part of his absence, Hester kept herself unusually busy. She practiced assiduously, working on duets with Ginny; she gave several bridge luncheons; she joined groups going to the city for matinees, not knowing, once there, what she was seeing. Then, at last, she knew what besides Justin she was missing. It was Sackville. What was the chorus doing now? What of the cadets and Liz, after her triumph? Hester blamed herself: she too, had been selfish. She could not fill his place but she could let them know she cared.

It was a blustery day when she set forth, driving slowly,

for the snow was deep in places, but at last she drew up at the schoolhouse and waited until she thought it was time for the older boys to be dismissed. She got out of the car and met them as they came. With a whoop they surrounded her. "It's Mrs. Carr! It's Mrs. Carr!" they shouted to each other. Bony even touched the fur of her coat with a none-too-clean hand.

They plied her with questions about Justin, which she parried as best she could.

"He came here the day after the show an' walked 'round an' saw everybody an' told us all how good we'd done an' shook hands an' all, an' then we never seen him again before we heard he'd left town. It ain't reasonable, Mrs. Carr, for him to act like that!" said Bony, still absent-mindedly smoothing her coat.

"But we know about Bill Hoover takin' your pup, the dirty skunk. An' one of Bill's kids said he an' Mr. Justin had high words when you all went to get the dog."

"An' why did Bill make such a hellfire stink about Mr. Justin's bein' born in Sackville?" 'Loyshus wanted to know. "We like that. Makes him seem like one of us, don't it now, Mrs. Carr?"

Hester swallowed bravely. "Yes, I'm sure you would all feel that way."

"Well, when's he comin' back? That's what's bitin' us all. We try to keep on practicin' but it don't seem like we get anywhere. He was even talkin' once of an open air grandstand or somethin' where we could give concerts like on Decoration Day an' Fourth of July. He just spoke about it that once but we was all excited. We just thought after the show we'd start in on them things an' it would be fun."

"An' where's our suits? Nobody seems to know. I want them suits kep' safe an' not lost nor nothin'." Bony's tone was belligerent.

"I'll tell you," Hester said. " 'Loyshus' mother has them all folded up in a bureau drawer. She told me Mr. Justin had asked her to take care of them and the girls' robes until they were needed."

Bony's eyes were wary and also disillusioned. "An' when has Mr. Justin got so thick with Liz?" he asked, with a shade of bitterness in his tone.

Hester motioned them to come closer. "I'll tell you a secret, but you needn't say too much about it. 'Loyshus' mother is Mr. Justin's sister. He never saw her face to face until the night of the show. She had recognized him but was shy about letting him see her. But after her solo — yes, she was the singer."

For a moment, the boys said nothing in their amazement, then 'Loyshus strutted before them, thumbs in his armpits.

"Get a load of *me,* you cats! Mr. Justin's my uncle! Ain't he, Mrs. Carr?"

"Yes, 'Loyshus. But I wouldn't boast about it. He's fond of all you boys. And now here's what I thought about your practice. If I come down just as I used to and accompany you and the girls, would that make a difference?"

"It sure would," the boys agreed boisterously, one after the other.

"The girls are keepin' on but they hardly sing anything but that 'Londonderry Air' thing, I s'pose because *he* liked it an' we're so sick of it we could puke," said Bony the Poet. "Here they come now. I made new words for it an' we all sing it at them." Loud and clear now rose the boyish voices as the girls approached.

> Would God I never hear the chorus singin',
> Until they're nearly out of breath,
> About a damned green apple blossom
> Till we could choke them *even until death!*

The closing words came in a volley of sound while the girls hurried to Hester, who, overcome by her own amusement, had difficulty sympathizing with them.

"We have to put up with that. Mr. Brown just laughs, but Mr. Justin would stop them quick enough. Oh, Mrs. Carr, when is he coming back?"

"I don't know," she replied, choosing her words carefully. "I think he probably had business to attend to up at his college."

"You think he'll come *sometime,* don't you? Nothing seems the same when he's not in and out."

"I know," Hester said sadly, adding under her breath, "too well." Then she began to make plans.

It was settled at last that she would come to accompany the boys Tuesdays after school, checking with Mr. Brown. Thursday would be the girls' day and she promised to hunt up some new songs for them. Also, in her mind, she decided to have them at her house once at least, if the weather moderated, to give them a taste of the gentler side of life. The boys she would not undertake without Justin. So often, she thought of what she could not do *without him.*

As she drove slowly back that afternoon she felt better, however; she was keeping the children interested, she was carrying on Justin's work and she was finding release from the tension of her own heart. When she got home she played with Flushie, laughed as she quoted Bony's rhyme to Hattie and chatted of the plans. Hattie was most agreeable.

"Well, it's good to see you takin' a little interest in life again. I do believe the pup here has been sort of pinin' away too. Look at him. I tell you, he's *thin.* Oh, here's a letter for you."

"Hattie, I've asked you always to lay mail on the tray on the hall table where I can see it at once."

"I do put the rest there, but if there's one from *him,* I just feel it to see if it's any thicker than usual an' I let Flushie smell it. He always barks an' wants to lick it an' it can do no harm to give the poor beast that little satisfaction."

Hester had noticed the dog's reaction to the letters herself. Somehow it made her more lonely than ever. This present one was much like the others except for one sentence. *The enemy daily shows signs of retreat. I don't deserve quarter, but if I win —*

Hester slept better that night, after making plans to visit more with Liz and Snecky. The practices went amazingly well. Both boys and girls seemed to labor under the conviction that the better they performed, the sooner their idol would return to them. Ginny often took over the girls. They liked her and her racy humor and recognized her sure touch on the piano as they did Hester's. New music in sheet form appeared with professional-looking covers, adding greatly, the girls felt, to their prestige over the boys. But they too had something about which to brag — music stands provided by some good angel! So general enthusiam was high, at least as high as could be maintained without their leader.

One night near the end of February when Hester answered the knocker, she found Tom Masters standing there alone, a wide smile on his face.

"Why Tom! Where's Ginny? Come in."

"I'm on strictly official business, so Ginny wasn't welcome. But I'll certainly come in. I've got some important news." He looked at her keenly while her cheeks flamed.

"Yes," he said to her unspoken question, as he shed his coat in the hall, "it has to do with Justin."

He seated himself comfortably, drew some papers from his briefcase and started his story.

"First of all I must tell you that Dr. Howard's prayers have worked another miracle all right. A new wave of feeling has swept over Westbrook. It began, of course, with the show. Before that nobody thought any good could come out of Sackville, but all at once, they found they had been mistaken. Then after the show" — he stopped and looked keenly at Hester — "you know what happened then was a bitter thing for any man to take. The dirty way Bill Hoover brought out the details. And up here, you know, not a man shook his hand, except me. Well, I've thought about how I'd feel in the same circumstances and you know what I concluded?"

"What?" Hester asked faintly.

"I think I'd have gotten the hell out of here, just as he did. For a while, that is. 'Till I'd gotten a new perspective on myself and given the town a chance to recover from the news."

Hester only looked at him in amazement, but he was going on with his story.

"So, as I say, emotions ran high. At first it was shock.

Then gradually, everyone who knew him began to miss Justin and to feel pretty small when they thought of Sackville. We remembered all the articles we'd read and the fine speeches we'd listened to on anti-racism and togetherness and so on, and we sort of stood condemned. At last, at our Men's Club meeting — you know, the members are pretty representative — Laird made a motion that they appoint me as secretary to write Justin to come back and there wasn't a dissenting vote even from the biggest hoity-toity there! Then I played my trump card. Want to hear?"

"You know I do," Hester said, her eyes swimming.

"Well, before I left for the meeting, I had two of your kids for callers. The ones you call Bony and 'Loyshus. I suppose their mothers knew how to direct them for they've worked for Ginny. When I heard what they'd come for I took them along and smuggled them into the coat room at the Club. I never dreamed then about the vote. But right after that I brought in the boys and let them tell their story."

"Oh, Tom! What on earth did they say?"

"They stood there in front of everybody as cool and collected as you please and this Bony explained that they had all decided that the reason Mr. Justin had gone away was because he was ashamed he'd been born in Sackville and so they were going to clean up the whole stinkin' mess (his words) and make it a place *anybody* would be *glad* to be born in."

"Oh, the darlings!" Hester murmured.

"Then, this 'Loyshus put in that they'd talked about it to Bostwick and he'd given them several rakes and hoes and as soon as the snow was gone, they'd start in leveling off the road and cleaning up the debris generally. But it was the trees, he said, bothered them. If they just had trees, Sackville would look as nice as any place. But how did you get *trees?* That's what they'd come to find out.

"Well, you should have seen those solid citizens watching the boys as they were laying it all on the line before them. There wasn't a trace of self-consciousness in those kids. God, they'd be great in the movies. But heaven save them from that. However, the men were so impressed that they kept shooting questions at them until one man said, 'I'll give a tree and see that it's planted!' And then another spoke up and another until every man jack of us had promised one. This 'Loyshus, with a pencil and a dirty piece of tablet paper, was carefully keeping count and at last he yelled, 'That'll do it! That'll go right down the whole damned street, I'm tellin' you!' The men roared with laughter and a state of euphoria prevailed as the kids thanked them and took off. Well, now for the letter."

He drew the sheet toward him and read:

DEAR JUSTIN:

The Men's Club here at their last meeting deputized me as their secretary to write you that, by a unanimous vote, they had indicated their desire to have you return, as soon as convenient, to Westbrook. They wish to express their respect for you and their admiration for the work you have already done. They hope that, once back among us, you can, as it were, monitor our consciences a little and help us develop something of the spirit of brotherhood.

Very sincerely yours,

"What do you think of it?"

"It's wonderful! It's perfect! Oh, Tom, that will heal all his hurts."

"That's what we hope. I added a postscript of my own. Don't know whether to read you that or not." He paused. "Well, why the devil shouldn't I? You'll understand it better than anyone else could except Justin himself."

He turned to a fresh page and read:

> Of course, I wouldn't dream of intruding upon your private and personal affairs, I would just like to state, unequivocally, that I think you're a damned fool!

"That ought to fix him!" Tom said complacently and then, "Why Hester, my dear girl, what's the matter?"

For Hester was crying. Not mild weeping, but racking breaths which she couldn't control. Tom watched her a few minutes judicially and then patted her gently on the head, got his coat and prepared to leave.

"You need to let go, Hester. Best thing you can do. You've been brave and put up a good front for a long time. Now, just expect the best for I'm sure it's coming. This letter will go out in the morning and I think it will bring results. Don't get up. Ginny will call you later. Good night, my dear!"

And Hester wept on, unrestrainedly, until all the long tension left her body and her mind also. She felt weak and relaxed and at peace. When Hattie came down to check the doors, she looked at her mistress in surprise.

"An' what's wrong with you now? Wasn't that Tom Masters I heard down here? What did he do to set you off like this?"

Hester knew her smile must look idiotic but she couldn't help it. "I'm just all at once so — so happy!" And the sobs began again.

"Well, you've a queer way of showin' it, but I'll make you a nice hot toddy an' that will fettle you. Come on, Flushie. Go seek the kitties, then you can both get on to bed."

Hester sipped her drink slowly and felt steadier. Her hands must stop trembling for she too intended to write a letter, different from any she had previously sent. Later, at the desk in her room, she penned it carefully.

DEAR, DEAR JOHN:

This is to tell you that my own particular enemy (which may be the same as yours) is entirely routed. Its name is *pride* and in love there is no place for that. So, laying all womanly reserve aside, I beg you to come back to me.

She signed it, sealed it, looked lovingly at it as though the words of it had been actually spoken and received, then slipped beneath the soft blankets of her bed and slept as she had not done since the dreadful night of Bill Hoover's disclosure.

CHAPTER EIGHT

AND JUST WHEN Tom Masters was developing a worried wrinkle in his forehead and Hester's sudden happy hopes were becoming clouded with doubt — Justin came back!

February had roared its cold and blustering way and departed. Nature, as though to make amends for its harshness, sent March in, not only as a lamb, but as such a mild and a gentle one that everybody marveled and Hattie spoke darkly of 'pet' days that boded ill for later weather. So it was on a late afternoon, balmy and warm, when windows were being opened for the spring air, that Justin knocked at Hester's door and when she came, stood waiting, hesitant, his eyes devouring her, until her outstretched hands drew him in. Then he waited no longer but took her at last in his arms.

After the kisses which left her breathless, he raised his head. "You see now, don't you, why I couldn't take just *one* and stop there?"

"But I've never been kissed like this before!"

"You haven't? Of course I'm glad. But why?"

She spoke shyly. "I don't think there was any real passion in my marriage."

He drew her closer and laid his cheek against hers. "I'm afraid, darling, you'll have to be prepared for a great deal in ours."

There was the sudden opening of the door between dining room and kitchen and a small hurricane streaked into the hall. Flushie, forgetting all former reprimands, leaped upon Justin, licking his hands, trying to reach his face, barking furiously to show his joy. Hattie followed, wide-eyed, but with evident effort to maintain her composure.

"Well, Mr. Justin, an' a sight for sore eyes you are. Just by luck I've got your favorite dinner too. It sort of run in my head you'd be comin'. Just tell me when you want it served, Miss Hester, and — "

She watched, startled as Justin drew her mistress closer to him and then said wonderingly, "So you've *spoke* at last!"

Hester blushed and Justin laughed as he looked down at her. "I think I've made my feelings quite clear, Hattie, so you needn't worry about that."

"And please, let's have dinner at once. I'm starved and I don't imagine Mr. Justin has had anything yet to eat."

"Nary a bite nor a sup! I was hoping, shamelessly, to get here in time."

At the table any real conversation was made impossible by Flushie's exuberant behavior and by Hattie's constant entrances on one pretext or another as though fearful the guest might have vanished. But, at last, Justin and Hester were alone in the drawing room. Here, he did not sit down at once beside her, but walked over to the north window and stood, his back to her, looking out at the early spring twilight.

"I'm sure," he said at last, very low, "that you know I love you with my very soul. I think it began that first night at the Masters' dinner. But then the vague, haunting feeling that we must have met before kept teasing at my mind, keeping other thoughts at bay. Later, the memory was clear, as you know, and then so was my love."

He stood still a little longer and then turning, came to her. His face was very grave. "Hattie's words reminded me that I haven't asked you the question I had been so burning to ask that dreadful night I left you. I want to put it in words. Knowing all my past, will you marry me, Hester?"

She gave a soft laugh. "That is the most superfluous question I ever heard, but I like your putting it to me in the real conventional form. Yes, John, a thousand times, *yes.*"

Then they settled close in the embraces for which Hester knew her heart had unconsciously been longing over the years.

There was, indeed, a great deal to talk about. Justin wanted an early wedding and they both agreed upon telling Dr. Howard soon so that a date could be set. Of course, Ginny and Tom Masters would help with details.

"I stopped at their door as I came by and announced my

return, for I had left him an extra key to the house. Also, I had a letter from him in the name of the Men's Club, urging me to come back. That did heal some bruises, I tell you. Also, I had an amazing missive from Bony, made up of common sense and profanity in about equal parts, but managing to tell me the plans for cleaning up Sackville and of how much they missed me. I believe I shed a tear or two over that one." He paused. "And then I had a letter from you. Which of the three sent me hurrying to finish up a few odds and ends I'd been helping with at the college, pack my bag and start back? Which of the three?"

"Bony's," Hester murmured faintly.

"Dear little liar," he said tenderly. "Don't ever try to dissemble from me for I can read you like a book. It was silly of me to ask that question even in fun. Your letter was the sweetest bit of writing I've ever had in my life and I intend to keep it always. Save it for our children."

She raised a startled, radiant face. "Why, John, I never once thought — we really *might* have a — a — "

"I've heard it frequently happens," he said calmly, "but don't let's get involved in future possibilities now. We've so many present plans to work out. Would you like to go abroad on a honeymoon?"

"Love it!"

"What about shipboard if there's a good one still running?"

"Wonderful! I hate flying."

"I'll look into the matter at once. If we go that way we can live over our first meeting! Wouldn't that be fun?"

"It would be sweet," she said.

"That is the truer word. Thank you for it. Now, as to the practical matters of living. I like my teaching job very much, but since I've been here I've discovered how very much more I enjoy writing. I've almost finished the book I was working at, but two others are beating at the bars to get done, so I suppose I could keep on. The important thing is which sort of life you feel you would prefer. The college atmosphere, which is really quite pleasant, though a little narrow, or your usual one here in Westbrook. I will be content with either. It is your choice."

"Oh, I'd rather stay here if you would like it."

"Yes, I would. I had begun to chafe a bit at ivied walls and their present problems. But now, as to our home. I would feel a bit embarrassed just to come in here and hang my hat, when I'm perfectly able to buy or build you whatever sort of house your heart might desire. Please be frank about this."

Hester spoke slowly. "I love this house. It is far from small, as you know, but it's still capable of enlargement. I've often wanted to extend the library and make a music room at the back. I would rather work there than here at the front on my own things, and since your violin practice has come along so well, we could enjoy the room ourselves and even have small musicales for our friends now and then."

"Wonderful!" Justin exclaimed. "I couldn't be happier than to live here with you. It's the nearest thing to home I've had in many years. Thank you, darling."

"One thing more. There's a good-sized dressing room opening out of my bedroom which you could easily use as a study and a quiet place for your writing."

She watched him anxiously. "Anything wrong?"

"Well, it's just this. If I live here with you, will old memories make any sort of barrier between us?"

She smiled and then answered him gently. "Never. The memories I thought I had have all melted away. Since I've known you, I've realized that they never did have substance. I've never actually loved anyone but you, John, so set your mind at rest."

It was a long time before they spoke again. After that, suddenly, the hour was late and Justin pretended fear of Hattie if he stayed longer. But much had been settled. They would be married in St. Paul's and Justin would speak to Dr. Howard in the morning. There would be no engraved invitations, just informal word-of-mouth ones to their closest friends of Westbrook, and as to Sackville, it was thought wisest to do as they had done for the show, simply pass the news along and say that anyone who cared to come was welcome, with a special message to Bostwick.

"And no reception?" Hester had asked a little wistfully.

"I'm afraid not, darling. It might be too complicated. Why couldn't we stand in the vestibule after the ceremony — I'll see there are plenty of flowers there and light — and shake hands with all who want to speak to us and then leave. When we get back from our trip, we can have a bang-up party at the Country Club and no feelings hurt."

"Perfect," Hester had agreed.

As he was leaving after his last embrace, he turned at the door and looked at her as she stood with the hall light on her hair. "You're so gentle, dearest, I must look out for that. You have taken all my suggestions without any question. You musn't do that later on. You must fly at me sometimes. I don't think I'm a masterful sort of man, but it could be heady business to be married to a docile wife. And here is the ceremony coming up with Dr. Howard, old-fashioned as they make them. He'll expect to keep the *obey* in the service and I don't think I'd like you to promise that!"

"Nonsense!" Hester said. "As though it could make any difference between us. I'm really a strong-minded woman, but I'll do this. When I go up to my room, I'll write in my little notebook, *Occasional temper tantrums requested.* Will that satisfy you?"

So when Hattie peered over the balustrade to see if the coast was clear to come down to close up the house, she found them both laughing hilariously.

As Tom Masters told him next day, Justin had managed to stir up the town one way or another ever since he first arrived there. Now the present excitement was, by all agreement, the best. Of course, Tom would be proud to be best man and Ginny was so sure of her own part in the proceedings, she was already ordering her dress. But, most delightful of all, she was having the opportunity of spreading the news to all her friends. It was amazing how quickly the plans fell into place. Dr. Howard was full of beatitudes as Justin explained Hester's wishes and his own in connection with Sackville.

"Ah," said the good man. "No one can deny anyone the right to the church itself. This, then, will fulfill an old desire of mine. The rich and the poor shall meet together. The Lord is the maker of them all. Has Mrs. Carr planned for music?" he added.

"I don't believe so," Justin said. "We have thought of a very simple service under the conditions."

"What conditions?" Dr. Howard asked. "Two people loving each other and wishing to marry fulfill all conditions. I prefer to have music at a wedding, myself. What about 'O Perfect Love'?"

"I don't believe I know it, in song, that is," he amended, grinning.

Dr. Howard chuckled. "Good. It should be sung at every wedding. What about having the woman with the marvelous voice who sang the Christmas solo sing it just before the benediction."

Justin stiffened. "If you mean Lib — Liz, as she is called — she is my sister."

"How nice," the Doctor said calmly. "Will you ask her or shall I?"

"Your — your *vestry?*"

"The parish house and all the secular adjuncts to the church are indeed under the care of the vestry. But the *Sanctuary* itself, I rather like to think is under my own jurisdiction. There will be no criticism from anyone who heard that wonderful voice in the Christmas show nor from anyone else, I feel sure. Wouldn't you like it?"

"More than I can say. But Lib is very shy."

"She can slip in at the choir entrance into one of the back stalls and hardly be noticed. As a matter of fact, she could even sing without rising, for you two will be kneeling at the altar just before the benediction. Would Mrs. Carr be willing to leave the music arrangements to me and the choirmaster? We work well together."

"I'm sure she would be most happy to do that."

"Then I'll try to make this a beautiful wedding. Just one stipulation. I want you to give me a promise."

"Anything!"

"Not so fast. Wait till you hear."

"I'll take a chance."

"I want you to give me your word that from now on you will not use *prayer,* as you said, only as a last resort."

Justin looked startled, thought for a moment and then held out his hand. "I promise, sir."

"Good. In a sense that is my clergyman's wedding gift to you and your bride."

That night, Justin said suddenly, "Darling, did you ever hear a song called 'O Perfect Love'?"

"Of course, it's often sung at weddings. Why?"

"Because Dr. Howard has the idea of getting Lib to sing it at ours."

She looked at him in amazement.

"He thinks," Justin went on, "that he can persuade her to do it and would like to take over the music along with the choirmaster if you are willing. Are you?"

"Of course, but might this not make trouble, *in the church?*"

"He thinks not. Says the Sanctuary is his domain rather than the vestry's."

"If he can do this, would it mean much to you?"

"More than I can say."

"And to me too. I'll play the hymn for you and try to sing the words, though you know I haven't much voice." She went quickly to the piano and felt for the key. "I know the first verse by heart." Justin stood close as she sang.

> O perfect Love, all human thought transcending,
> Lowly we kneel in prayer before Thy throne,

> That theirs may be the love which knows no ending,
> Whom thou forevermore dost join in one.

"The other verses are equally beautiful, but I don't remember them. I'll look them up for you, though."

Justin's eyes were wet. "Wonderful. It's as though it were just made for us. I only hope Lib will agree to sing it."

Even as he spoke, they heard a knock on the back door which Flushie rushed, barking, to answer, then Hattie's voice as she calmed the dog and came through to the doorway.

"It's Liz, Mr. Justin. I mean, Lib, and she wants to see you special and as quick as you can."

Justin hurried to the kitchen where Lib waited. "Oh Johnny, it's Snecky. He's just had a cold, I thought, but yesterday it went into his chest an' today I was scared and sent 'Loyshus for the doctor over in the Row. So he come an' — an' he says it's pneumonia an' gone deep already. Snecky's all the time askin' for you. Could you come, Johnny?"

"Of course. At once. Wait, I'll tell Hester. Then I'll take you back in my car."

"I'm so scared," Lib kept saying through her tears. "He's been kind to me an' the kids. If he — if he don't get well, I'll be so lost. I'll have no one."

"You'll have me, Lib. I'll always see to you and the children. I promise you will have enough money to live decently, and I have other plans for you all as well. I know you'll grieve for Snecky, but don't feel despairing. I'll miss him, too," he added.

When they reached the house, they could hear at once

the labored breathing and sharp little coughs. Justin went at once to Snecky's room and leaned over the bed. He took the old man's thin hands in his own.

"Snecky!" he said. "I'm distressed you are sick. Is there anything I can do for you?"

"Yes. Talk to me. Tell me how the kids are doin'." His mind seemed to wander. After a few minutes he said, "It's mebbe only done for generals and sichlike, but I'd like so cruel well to have drum sounds at my funeral."

"No, Snecky, you're going to get better. Don't talk that way."

The old man slowly shook his head. "I ask the doctor plain an' he told me plain. But kind. Very kind. I guess I'm near the end of my *Providential way,* Mr. Justin. An' somehow I sort of accept it all if you'll just look after the family."

His voice dropped and his eyelids closed. Justin leaned closer.

"You can hear me, Snecky?"

The old man nodded.

"I'll take care of them, and about the drums — I'll see to that myself. You understand?"

Snecky smiled and then seemed to sink into sleep. Justin rose and loosed the thin hands from his own. He went out to where Lib and her children were sitting, tears on their cheeks, at the kitchen table. He put a touch like a caress upon the shoulder of each.

"He is asleep," he said, "and I have a feeling, a hope, that he may not wake." He laid a little roll of bills beside Lib. "You must let me know what you need," he said, "and

I'll be down in the morning. Or would it help if I stayed to-night and sat up with Snecky?"

"Me and the children will do that. We'll take turns, but thank you, Johnny. Just to know you're near is such a big relief. An' the neighbors are good. The men will know just what to do if— if anything happens."

When Justin was once again in Hester's drawing room, he told her all the story, ending with Snecky's request for the drums at his funeral.

"That touched me. I told him I would see to it. What the boys have learned would not be very appropriate for the occasion, so I think I'll do it."

Hester looked at him, wide-eyed. "Why John, you don't mean to say you can beat a drum?"

He laughed. "My dearest, did you really think I would attempt to start a drum corps if I couldn't beat a drum my-self?"

"I never gave it a thought."

"And apparently no one else did either. But, yes, I'm a drummer from way back. Military school, you see, in my teens. I did pretty well academically, but my great thrill was in being the best at the drums. I'm mad about them. I brought my own big one along and have practiced when I thought no one would hear. This was my idea."

He stopped to smile into Hester's puzzled eyes. "Of course, I would have trained the boys and loved it, but I felt if there should happen to be one man in their town who knew drums and would take over the kids, it would be so much better. All Sackville then, you see. Well, Snecky was simply born for the job and you know what it meant to him and the boys too. I let him do the ground work and I supervised the practice. You'll never know how hard it was for me to keep my hands off the sticks, but it was all worth it."

"And you'll really play the drums for Snecky's funeral?"

"Yes, I promised, so I'll do my best. My last gift to him."

She laid her hand on his. "You're a good man, John."

"No," he said, considering, as his arms went round her, "I don't think I am really, but between you and Dr. Howard, maybe I'll get better."

The next morning when he went down to the house he found, as he had expected, that Snecky had quietly completed his Providential way in the night and the neighbors had already taken over the duties that, time out of mind, had been a part of their self-contained handling of both life and death. When he asked Lib about a service, her reddened eyes looked frightened.

"Oh Johnny, I don't think Snecky would have wanted anything like that! You see, nobody goes to church the way you would mean. I'll tell you, Johnny, what to do. Talk to Mr. Kirk next door. He liked Snecky and he's sort of takin' charge of things for me."

Justin knelt for a moment beside Snecky's quiet bed and then went to see Mr. Kirk, who proved to be a large, florid man with a thin little wife and what seemed to be quite a number of small children underfoot. He listened politely to Justin's hesitant questions about the services of a minister for Snecky. Then he laughed.

"Naw, we ain't a churchgoin' town somehow. Every once in a while a ripsnortin' evangelist comes here an' stays a few days preachin' hellfire and everybody goes just for something to do. Then there's a Methodist preacher stops by an' a Catholic priest once in a while an' that's the amount of it. Snecky never took much to preachin'. What we do at a funeral, we all just fall into line an' march down to the little graveyard beside the church an' that's all, Mr. Justin. Better not try to change it."

"I won't," Justin said promptly. "But I know a nice clergyman who I think would be willing to march along and then just give a final benediction at the grave. That would be all. What do you think?"

"Well, that sounds all right to me. Just something a little extry for Snecky. We all thought an awful lot of him."

So it was arranged. Dr. Howard jostled a few notes on his calendar and agreed to do his part. Justin explained to his young drummers what he intended to do and they looked at him with awe.

"An' all this time we never knowed it," Bony said.

"Then you'll be our teacher from now on?"

"As soon as I get home from my wedding trip."

"Hot diggity! Will it be long?"

"I'll be back in time to start practice for Memorial Day."

The weather was still mild the next afternoon when the procession formed in Sackville. The strongest men carrying the burden, a light one, on their shoulders, came first; then Dr. Howard in his vestments; then Justin with the great drum strapped across his shoulders and then practically the whole populace of Sackville, many out of respect for Snecky and some out of curiosity when they saw the clergyman and Justin, and close behind, Lib with her children, weeping.

When Mr. Kirk gave the signal, Justin began the funeral march for his old friend. Softly at first, then louder with incredible changes and flourishes, until it seemed that the drum actually played a melody. To the steady throb, the people marched until the bearers set down their burden. Justin beat a soft tattoo and then as the men stood with their worn hats on their breasts and many of the women cried quietly, Dr. Howard's clear voice reached even to the edge of the crowd as he read, with tenderness, a few short prayers and then pronounced the benediction.

As they all turned back, Justin was amazed at the response of the people both to the drumming and to Dr. Howard.

"That was wonderful, Mr. Justin. You give Snecky a proper sendoff. That you did."

"Yes, that was a fine thing you done for Snecky, Mr. Justin. Wish't he could have heard it!"

"An', Reverend, we liked what you done, just simple an' quiet-like. If we could have a preacher like you once in a while I think we'd go to church."

"You can have me sometimes if you want me. I would be happy to come. Is your church in good repair?"

The men looked at each other. "Well," Kirk said, "I wouldn't just say that, but if a few of us fellows got at it, we could fix it up all right."

"Good," said Dr. Howard. "When you get it ready, let me know and I'll come and give you a service. A quiet one," he added, smiling.

It was the night before the wedding. There had been a brief rehearsal before dinner, chiefly to arrange for the unusual part of the service which was that Hester, having no one to give her away, would walk up the aisle with Justin, with Ginny leading them; Tom would join them at the chancel where Dr. Howard would also be waiting. The latter had told Justin quietly that Lib had agreed to sing the wedding hymn if she could sit unseen at the back of the choir stalls. And the choirmaster who was training her had told him he was overcome by the beauty of her voice.

Justin gave a few more instructions to the three Sackville boys who were to help the Westbrook men usher and a parting word to the florist who had dropped in for a final check.

"Don't forget. We want a lovely white bouquet at the end of every pew," he said. Then in an aside to Ginny, "That will mean more to the Sackville guests than anything else."

They all parted at the church door with assurances that the incredibly mild weather was going to hold out for the morrow, and with laughter and good wishes, all went home.

At dinner that evening, Hattie was irrepressible. "An' Mr. Justin, I'm tellin' you, her dress looks exactly like a bride's!"

"Well, that's what I'll be," Hester said.

"Oh, you know what I mean. It ain't really white, but it's so close to it as makes no difference an' she looks like a dream in it," Hattie added.

"A dream," he said softly, "and I won't actually believe it *isn't* a dream until I've got the ring on her finger."

Hester turned her beautiful diamond back and forth on her otherwise ringless hand. "It's so perfectly lovely. I've never been able to thank you properly but it means so much to me."

"I hope you will like the more important one as well."

Before dinner was over Justin gave a quick exclamation. "Oh," he said, "I forgot to tell you something important. I had a letter from Mac!"

"John, you didn't! What did he say?"

"Well, the news was interesting. One of the men to whom I sent him evidently took a liking to the boy and found him a job and some sort of a room. Now he's working every day and going to school at night. Could anything be better?"

"John, you don't think he might — ?"

"I'm not looking into the future but I have faith in that boy and the present looks good. So let's leave it there."

They went out on the front steps in the gentle early-evening air. From the street above them came the sound of children's voices at a game.

"Listen!" Hester said. "It's probably a birthday party and it's warm enough to be outside. They're singing "The Farmer in the Dell." You know it, don't you?"

"I'm afraid I don't remember it."

"Oh, it goes:

> The farmer takes a wife
> The wife takes a child
> The child takes the nurse
> The nurse takes the dog

and so on." Then she began to laugh. I don't believe you know what a big part Flushie has played in our romance."

"Tell me all of it. I'll appreciate him even more then."

"Well," Hester began, "it was like this. I was walking up the street one spring day — just before you had been in town long — feeling very sad and lonely. I suddenly heard the children singing this song game and the line *The nurse takes the dog* struck me, for Ginny had been after me to get one. That night — this was funny — I woke myself saying *The lady takes a dog!* and then I began to sing it, laughing to myself. The very next day, Ginny appeared to take me to the kennels and I got Flushie. What do you think about that?"

"A charming coincidence."

"But you haven't heard it all. That night we made a little bed for him in the kitchen, but I woke up about three o'clock with the sound of pathetic little moans from below so I hurried down to get him and bring him up with me. As I was crossing the hall, here, with him, I glanced out the glass panel in the door. There, plainly in the moonlight and the street light too, I saw a man standing in front of my house just staring in at it. I was terrified for Ginny had told me of the nightly marauder. Then, as I looked — this seems incredible after the years — but I recognized you. You see, your face, John, hasn't really changed much. Older, but still thin and your hair is the same. So, my memory of that night on shipboard, which at the time had stirred me very much, strangely came back to me. I ran upstairs quickly to see if it persisted and it did."

He looked at her in amazement. "It doesn't seem possible. Yet, you were then at the most impressionable age. And even I, when I met you here, was at once haunted by the feeling we had somehow seen each other before. Well, all I say is, blessings on Flushie!"

"But there still is more. In all our friendship, as it grew closer and closer, he was always with us. It almost seemed as if he knew. Then the night he was stolen! That whole wretched business involving him brought about our dreadful separation and our utterly blissful reunion. Do you wonder I feel a great tenderness when I think of my line *The lady takes a dog.*"

Justin drew her closer. "No, darling, I don't wonder. I feel very touched myself but I must remind you of something else." His voice was low.

"What?" she whispered.

"Tomorrow you are going to take something much more important than a dog. You're going to take a *husband* too!"